11/21

On
Girlhood

ALSO BY GLORY EDIM

Well-Read Black Girl:
Finding Our Stories, Discovering Ourselves

On
Girlhood

15 Stories from the Well-Read Black Girl Library

Glory Edim

Liveright Publishing Corporation
A Division of W. W. Norton & Company
Independent Publishers Since 1923

Since this page cannot accommodate all the copyright notices,
pages 199–200 constitute an extension of the copyright page.

For information about special discounts for bulk purchases, please contact
W. W. Norton Special Sales at specialsales@wwnorton.com or 800-233-4830

Manufacturing by Lake Book Manufacturing
Book design by Chris Welch
Production manager: Anna Oler

ISBN 978-1-63149-769-8

Liveright Publishing Corporation, 500 Fifth Avenue, New York, N.Y. 10110
www.wwnorton.com

W. W. Norton & Company Ltd., 15 Carlisle Street, London W1D 3BS

1 2 3 4 5 6 7 8 9 0

For Black girls, now and always

All those books—another world—just waiting
At my fingertips.

—NIKKI GIOVANNI,
"My First Memory (of Librarians)"

Contents

Love

Self-Discovery

Epilogue

Introduction

> When I look back, I am so impressed again with the
> life-giving power of literature. If I were a young per-
> son today, trying to gain a sense of myself in the world,
> I would do that again by reading, just as I did when I
> was young. —MAYA ANGELOU

I can remember when I first fell in love with short stories. I was at Howard University studying journalism; the campus was my haven and I spent the majority of my time nestled in the stacks at Founders Library. I was twenty years old and it was the biggest library I'd ever been in. From its grand reading rooms to its iconic bell tower, I moved about the shelves and experienced history. Founders Library has been a meeting place for social activism since 1867. I felt sharply aware of the literary lineage that moved through the halls, a history that included the one and only Zora Neale Hurston. In that library, I read every word that Hurston ever wrote—*Dust Tracks on a Road*, *Jonah's Gourd Vine*, and of course, *Their Eyes Were Watching God*, written during her fieldwork in Haiti and considered her seminal text.

As I read nonstop, I was simultaneously searching for my "purpose." Like Hurston, I longed to explore and write the eloquent, tell-all version of my life. However, I was naïve and inexperienced—college was more studious and less adventurous than I imagined. So, I lived vicariously through the worlds she conjured through fiction. *"She had been getting ready for her great journey to the horizons in search of people,"* Hurston wrote in *Their Eyes Were Watching God.* *"It was important to all the world that she should find them, and they find her."*

Zora Neale Hurston was the beating heart of the Harlem Renaissance and studied the beauty of folklore in the Black South. Originally from Notasulga, Alabama, Hurston traveled for her writing to places such as Haiti, Jamaica, and Honduras—and she always invoked the boisterous spirit and voice of the people she encountered, seamlessly weaving acute details into her work. It was her short story "Sweat" that captured my attention and taught me to be unafraid of the challenges that were bound to happen in my life.

The story of a hardworking washerwoman and her husband, "Sweat" is a deceptively simple tale of good and evil, suffering and redemption, and reaping what you sow. Delia works tirelessly seven days a week in order to keep her home and is completely exhausted by her husband Sykes's constant physical and emotional abuse—as evidenced by his repeated pranking her with a rattlesnake. She laments that her life is nothing but *"work and sweat, cry and sweat, pray and sweat."* Delia finally finds the strength from within to confront Sykes and order him from their shared home. And yes, her husband faces the ill-fated consequences of his pranks. Although I was only a college student at the time, I fully empathized with Delia's urge to feel fully liberated. Written in 1926 for the first and only issue of *Fire!!* magazine, Hurston's palpable narrations illustrated the depth and meaning of the lived experiences of everyday Black folks; her writing stood firm in the power of language, and it became the source of my literary inspiration and self-determination. As eloquently stated by Hurston herself, *"I have the nerve to walk my own way, however hard, in my search for reality, rather than climb upon the rattling wagon of wishful illusions."*

After I read "Sweat," my curiosity led me to discover the first short story ever published by an African-American woman: Frances Ellen Watkins Harper's "The Two Offers." By the time she first published the story in 1859, Harper had already established herself as a popular and well-respected poet, lecturer, and activist. She wrote progressively about the plight of Black people, and most of her works centered on her abolitionist efforts. What gripped me most about "The Two Offers" was its premise. Although one of the protagonists shares Harper's abolitionist sensibilities, neither is identified as a Black woman, nor is the abolition of slavery the central concern of the text. Instead, the story is a meditation on marriage and education for women. The story foreshadows her unforgettable poetry, including "Aunt Chloe's Politics" and "Renewal of Strength," along with the more feminist writing that marked her monumental shift toward the suffrage movement, and her efforts to help organize the Black women's club movement.

As a college student, I was taken by how both Hurston and Harper expressed their social and political views through poetry, novels, and speeches. There was an urgency and fearlessness to their work. But something about the short story form in particular appealed to me. I loved how their words enveloped me, how intensely the Black women characters were discontented, fierce, questioning, confused, undone, brave, grieving, overcome. The preciseness of the writing, the powerful themes of identity. These were multidimensional depictions of Black girlhood and womanhood. I was hooked, and have remained so ever since. I added every story I could find to my personal collection and studied with rigor. I found these narratives stayed with me wholly formed, perhaps because they were the earliest narrative examples I encountered of Black feminism and liberation.

Now, my personal library is more than a collection of books. It's where my passions, anxieties, and aspirations are gathered. As a child growing up in Arlington, Virginia, I spent hours at the public library and not the bookstore. For my hardworking mother, books were too expensive to buy, but she understood their power and value. With her instruction, I went to the public library every single day after school. Very early on I understood the importance of treating books as valuable, long-lasting objects instead of disposable ones. At the library I learned how to take good care of my community and the books I borrowed from it. I didn't bend my pages or write notes in the margins. I did my best to protect each book, so it would last and be used by many people. Books were to be loved and cherished. People were to be treated with respect and approached with curiosity. Every time I read something new or made a new friend, I strengthened my imagination. I found fanciful book covers intriguing, but it was thoughtful, lively characters that kept me immersed. They beckoned me, becoming lifelong companions. To be honest, there were so many times I didn't want to return a library book. I wanted to keep the book forever. This was true the first time I read Toni Morrison's debut novel, *The Bluest Eye.*

It's a life-changing book for many Black girls. Morrison places her reader in a position where they can empathize with the protagonist, Pecola Breedlove. She is an eleven-year-old Black girl who believes that she is ugly and that having blue eyes would make her beautiful. Sensitive and delicate, she passively suffers the abuse of her mother, father, and classmates. She is lonely and imaginative. We are furious at her neglect. Morrison writes, "Anger is better. There is a sense of being in anger. A reality and presence. An awareness of worth. It is a lovely surging." We feel the surging and want her to be saved. Toni Morrison's groundbreaking work set the literary precedent for the in-depth study of Black girlhood.

It wasn't until I was about sixteen that I started to buy my own books at real-life bookstores. I can still remember the two purchases that kicked off my collection: *The Color Purple*, by Alice Walker, and *Jazz*, by Toni Morrison. *The Color Purple* showed me a woman's struggle for empowerment and personal liberation. The novel documents the traumas and gradual triumphs of Celie, a young Black girl in rural Georgia. She narrates her life and longings through painfully honest letters to God. *Jazz* taught me about longing and the complicated history of the Great Migration. It begins in the midst of a love triangle between characters Violet, Joe, and Dorcas. Immediately the reader is confronted with the great potency of Black love and unrequited desire. *"Don't ever think I fell for you, or fell over you. I didn't fall in love, I rose in it,"* Joe Trace says to Dorcas. I am still fixated by this line.

I continued to buy my own books in high school and then into college. I read insistently, looking for answers to questions I hadn't yet asked aloud. Lots more Morrison and Walker filled my bookshelves. Yet I never abandoned my love for public libraries.

Whether I was in the eighth grade or entering my freshman year in college, the wonderment of the stacks enthralled me. Libraries fostered my curiosity and sustained my commitment to learning. My personal library filled another significant, more spiritual need. By curating my bookshelf at home, I gave myself permission to build a sanctuary of sorts. An awe-inspiring shelf where I would spend hours discovering and dreaming about who I would become. Each book a good-faith effort to better understand my identity as a Black woman.

WITH THIS ANTHOLOGY, I'm seeking to illuminate the narrow space between Black girlhood and Black womanhood. This is not a finite list of stories on Black girlhood; it's simply a starting point. I want to attest to the worthiness of Black girls as they come of age—their need for protection, love, and freedom. This is something I've sought to do with my organization, Well-Read Black Girl, which works tirelessly to address and improve society by reading and reflecting on the works of Black women. When selecting a book for our nationwide book club, I'm drawn to the possibilities for individual expression within varied story lines and distinct characters. Ultimately, my hope is that each narrative reveals the complex exterior worlds and interior lives as experienced, imagined, and seen through the eyes of Black girls.

Today, decades after buying my first book, I feel so proud of the handpicked stories in this collection. They are short stories that have brought my life so much meaning, and I firmly believe each story is worthy of deep reflection and celebration. *When you look over your own library, who do you see?* For many Black and Brown readers, collecting stories that reflect our life experiences helps us create new, uninhibited worlds where we can fully control the narratives. As a student at Howard University I was looking for myself on the page. And that search has never ended. I continue to yearn for the mundane, the painful, and the beautiful—all the facets of one becoming. I look for stories to remind myself that no matter how the landscapes may change, we are all faced with the same issues when finding our purpose: issues of love, loss, self-doubt, morality, and everything else that makes life full of meaning.

In all fifteen stories in this collection, the authors use a myriad of young characters to convey the beauty of Black girlhood. They are undeniably ambitious and inspired. We see them evolving from naïve and reserved children to courageous and strong-willed individuals with hopes of building a better life for themselves. We see them stumble, struggle with loss of self, and make life-altering mistakes. Their stories are brave, honest, and at times heartbreaking. Most importantly, as a young Black woman, I saw myself in these narratives. I found characters whose resilience, independence, and inner strength greatly inspired me. I found my voice in characters who looked like me and spoke like me—overcoming hardships to define themselves. I found a sense of self-worth and fortitude. From Amina Gautier's "Dance for Me" to Edwidge Danticat's "Seeing Things Simply," there was a visceral connection.

What I find most moving about the short stories within is the subtlety of the writing, which often stands in stark contrast to the heaviness of the themes. In story after story, we can engage and interrogate stereotypes tied to Black girlhood, particularly how these authors reveal a richer interior life for their characters than mainstream narratives typically allow. In pushing past flat stereotypes, these stories invite the reader to fully appreciate the lives of ordinary Black girls and women, and acknowledge the resilience, dignity, and the unending strength of these characters. I find it difficult to deny the literary impact of short stories written by Black women.

Whether you read a short story written by Zora Neale Hurston or Toni Cade Bambara, the genre is a mastery of eloquence and resilience. With each rereading of the collection, I was hit with new revelations. And isn't that what girlhood embodies: an endless stream of new discoveries as one moves toward adulthood? This anthology's purpose is twofold: to produce and uplift a new generation of Black women, and to encourage them to write and reflect on their childhoods with great love, curiosity, and self-regard. The stories in this collection are significant because they allow us to witness the ways in which we love and nurture Black girls; by placing these stories in the same frame, we can see new intimacies, painful contradictions, and surprising connections.

As I write this, we are living in a deeply reflective moment in society. Black life is endlessly precarious due to structural racism. Yet we persist. Each narrative reminds us that Black girls deserve to live in a world where they are protected and nurtured so they can stand in the fullness of their identities. We can imagine and create new worlds committed to our liberation and freedom. The writers, undeniably extraordinary, strike a beautiful balance of truth, tenderness, and love. Regardless of the decade or generation, they recognize the need for a resolute affirmation for Black girlhood amidst depilating systems of oppression.

When we read Jamaica Kincaid's "Girl," the interior life of a Black woman is immediately apparent:

This is how you smile to someone you don't like too much;
this is how you smile to someone you don't like at all; this is
how you smile to someone you like completely; this is how
you set a table for tea; this is how you set a table for dinner;
this is how you set a table for dinner with an important
guest; this is how you set a table for lunch; this is how you
set a table for breakfast.

We are indebted to dedicated storytellers like Kincaid—resonant
voices who at the time were unaware of their singular impact.

Both remarkable and engaging, these stories shine a light on
Black luminaries in short fiction, such as Paule Marshall, Dorothy West, and Alice Walker, as well as debut contemporary writers like Alexia Arthurs and Camille Acker, both Well-Read Black
Girl book club alumnae. Although this anthology spans decades,
it is composed as a collage of heartfelt moments and thoughts.
As Gwendolyn Brooks writes in "We're the Only Colored People Here," "She was learning to love moments. To love moments
for themselves." Throughout the course of our lives, we experience moments when we feel as though we do not belong. For
Black women, these moments can be steeped in racial or gender discrimination. I selected these stories because each pio-
neering author questions the status quo. Their writing serves as
an emblem of social ailment and progress, proclaiming our full
existence. They fill a void and grant us powerful characters who
have agency and unyielding promise: girls who are unapologetic
and bold, who depart from the path.

These stories consistently return to the complicated inner
work that is required when confronted with the trials of shaping one's identity while contending with racism. They provide

a unique opportunity to explore the delicate balance between progression and precariousness within Black girlhood. The line is thin, and shrouded with uncertainty, but each narrative proclaims that Black girlhood matters. Perhaps readers will redefine their own ideas of whose stories are important within the literary canon. Here are stories of young Black women carrying the weight of their dreams, with fragile hope, with boundless enthusiasm, every character engaging in the courageous pursuit of love. The heroines keep rising, despite the challenges they encounter, and they discover defiant joy within themselves. It is a profound act of liberation and salvation.

I remember how painful my loneliness was as a child and what yearning for love felt like as a teenager. I can recall my tendency to be easily persuaded in high school, along with my curiosity and complete fascination with literature once I entered college. Navigating countless rejections. The eagerness and sheer excitement to make my mark on the world. Each story in this anthology has the power to make these feelings come rushing back, and they leave me in awe of how far I've come as a Black woman. The characters within may feel that familiar. They may remind you of a past self or who you are striving to become.

On Girlhood is divided into four sections: *Innocence, Belonging, Love,* and *Self-Discovery.* Some narratives are told through the prism of childhood perception; others highlight pivotal transitions into marriage or motherhood. In *Innocence,* Jamaica Kincaid's "Girl" reveals a mother offering advice to her daughter by listing rigid rules to abide by. Toni Morrison's "Recitatif" follows two precocious eight-year-old girls at the St. Bonaventure orphanage as they nurture an unexpected friendship. In

Belonging, Toni Cade Bambara's "The Lesson" addresses class inequality and describes the stark contrast between Black and white people in society. "Who We Are" by Camille Acker is filled with authentic dialogues that mirror the youthful sounds of Washington, D.C. In *Love*, Dana Johnson's "Melvin in the Sixth Grade" drops us in Los Angeles with a lovesick teen named Avery. And in *Self-Discovery*, "Seeing Things Simply" by Edwidge Danticat introduces us to Princesse, a young woman with a strong sense of self and a hunger to be fully seen. The collection closes with an essay from the formidable Zora Neale Hurston, because she too was once "a little colored girl" full of ambition and promise. The essay is provocative and reinforces the nuance of identity and belonging as a Black woman. She was a writer at the vanguard of a changing America who freely defined herself:

> At certain times I have no race, I am me. When I set my hat at a certain angle and saunter down Seventh Avenue, Harlem City, feeling as snooty as the lions in front of the Forty-Second Street Library, for instance . . . The cosmic Zora emerges. I belong to no race nor time. I am the eternal feminine with its string of beads.

The authors in this anthology skillfully use tone, dialect, and vivid artistic detail to beautifully capture the lives of young Black women. The unique stylistic choices I found in going back to these stories were a revelation for me; I believe their aim was to produce writing that would be relevant and important to a Black audience, that would compel readers to closely examine experiences both mundane and monumental. As you read, I hope the authors—from Toni Morrison to Gwendolyn Brooks to Paule Marshall—create a vivid picture in your mind, illuminating the vastness of Black girlhood and womanhood. I hope the stories sustain you and encourage you to build your own library that imagines a brighter, bolder future for those you love. May every story be a boundless, continual act of discovery.

Innocence

Girl

Jamaica Kincaid

Originally published in 1978

This is how you smile to someone you don't like too much; this is how you smile to someone you don't like at all; this is how you smile to someone you like completely.

Wash the white clothes on Monday and put them on the stone heap; wash the color clothes on Tuesday and put them on the clothesline to dry; don't walk barehead in the hot sun; cook pumpkin fritters in very hot sweet oil; soak your little cloths right after you take them off; when buying cotton to make yourself a nice blouse, be sure that it doesn't have gum on it, because that way it won't hold up well after a wash; soak salt fish overnight before you cook it; is it true that you sing benna in Sunday school?; always eat your food in such a way that it won't turn someone else's stomach; on Sundays try to walk like a lady and not like the slut you are so bent on becoming; don't sing benna in Sunday school; you mustn't speak to wharf-rat boys, not even to give directions; don't eat fruits on the street—flies will follow you; *but I don't sing benna on Sundays at all and never in Sunday school*; this is how to sew on a button; this is how to make a buttonhole for the button you have just sewed on; this is how to hem a dress when you see the hem coming down and so to prevent yourself from looking like the slut I know you are so bent on becoming; this is how you iron your father's khaki shirt so that it doesn't have a crease; this is how you iron your father's khaki pants so that they don't have a crease; this is how you grow okra—far from the house, because okra tree harbors red ants; when you are growing dasheen, make sure it gets plenty of water or else it makes your throat itch when you are eating it; this is how you sweep a corner; this is how you sweep a whole house; this is how you sweep a yard; this is how you smile to someone you don't like too much; this is how you smile to someone you don't like at all; this is how you smile to someone you like completely; this is how you set a table for tea; this is how you set a table for dinner; this is how you set a table for dinner with an important guest; this is how you set a table for lunch; this is how you set a table for breakfast; this is how to behave in the presence of men who don't know you very well, and this way they won't recognize immediately the slut I have warned you against becoming; be sure to wash every day, even if it is with your own spit; don't squat down to play marbles—you are not a boy, you know; don't pick people's flowers—you might catch something; don't throw stones at blackbirds, because it might not be a blackbird at all; this is how to make a bread pudding; this is how to make doukona; this is how to make pepper pot; this is how to make a good medicine for a cold; this is how to make a good medicine to throw away a child before it even becomes a child; this is how to catch a fish; this is how to throw back a fish you don't like, and that way something bad won't fall on you; this is how to bully a man; this is how a man bullies you; this is how to love a man, and if this doesn't work there are other ways, and if they don't work don't feel too bad about giving up; this is how to spit up in the air if you feel like it, and this is how to move quick so that it doesn't fall on you; this is how to make ends meet; always squeeze bread to make sure it's fresh; *but what if the baker won't let me feel the bread?*; you mean to say that after all you are really going to be the kind of woman who the baker won't let near the bread?

DISCUSSION QUESTIONS

1. Consider the title, "Girl," and how it works with the short story. Why do you think the author chose it?

2. After reading the short story, how would you describe the mother-and-daughter relationship?

3. How do you interpret the tone of this story? Is the speaker coming from a place of frustration or love—or something else?

4. Can you recall a speech or piece of advice you were given by a parent or guardian? How did it affect the way you behaved as a young person?

Recitatif

Toni Morrison

Originally published in 1982

We were eight years old and got F's all the time. Me because I couldn't remember what I read or what the teacher said. And Roberta because she couldn't read at all and didn't even listen to the teacher.

My mother danced all night and Roberta's was sick. That's why we were taken to St. Bonny's. People want to put their arms around you when you tell them you were in a shelter, but it really wasn't bad. No big long room with one hundred beds like Bellevue. There were four to a room, and when Roberta and me came, there was a shortage of state kids, so we were the only ones assigned to 406 and could go from bed to bed if we wanted to. And we wanted to, too. We changed beds every night and for the whole four months we were there we never picked one out as our own permanent bed.

It didn't start out that way. The minute I walked in and the Big Bozo introduced us, I got sick to my stomach. It was one thing to be taken out of your own bed early in the morning—it was something else to be stuck in a strange place with a girl from a whole other race. And Mary, that's my mother, she was right. Every now and then she would stop dancing long enough to tell me something important and one of the things she said was that they never washed their hair and they smelled funny. Roberta sure did. Smell funny, I mean. So when the Big Bozo (nobody ever called her Mrs. Itkin, just like nobody ever said St. Bonaventure)—when she said, "Twyla, this is Roberta. Roberta, this is Twyla. Make each other welcome." I said, "My mother won't like you putting me in here."

"Good," said Bozo. "Maybe then she'll come and take you home."

How's that for mean? If Roberta had laughed I would have killed her, but she didn't. She just walked over to the window and stood with her back to us.

"Turn around," said the Bozo. "Don't be rude. Now Twyla. Roberta. When you hear a loud buzzer, that's the call for dinner. Come down to the first floor. Any fights and no movie." And then, just to make sure we knew what we would be missing, "The Wizard of Oz."

Roberta must have thought I meant that my mother would be mad about my being put in the shelter. Not about rooming with her, because as soon as Bozo left she came over to me and said, "Is your mother sick too?"

"No," I said. "She just likes to dance all night."

"Oh," she nodded her head and I liked the way she understood things so fast. So for the moment it didn't matter that we looked like salt and pepper standing there and that's what the other kids called us sometimes. We were eight years old and got F's all the time. Me because I couldn't remember what I read or what the teacher said. And Roberta because she couldn't read at all and didn't even listen to the teacher. She wasn't good at anything except jacks, at which she was a killer: pow scoop pow scoop pow scoop.

We didn't like each other all that much at first, but nobody else wanted to play with us because we weren't real orphans with beautiful dead parents in the sky. We were dumped. Even the New York City Puerto Ricans and the upstate Indians ignored us. All kinds of kids were in there, black ones, white ones, even two Koreans. The food was good, though. At least I thought so. Roberta hated it and left whole pieces of things on her plate: Spam, Salisbury steak—even jello with fruit cocktail in it, and she didn't care if I ate what she wouldn't. Mary's idea of supper was popcorn and a can of Yoo-Hoo. Hot mashed potatoes and two weenies was like Thanksgiving for me.

It really wasn't bad, St. Bonny's. The big girls on the second floor pushed us around now and then. But that was all. They wore lipstick and eyebrow pencil and wobbled their knees while they watched TV. Fifteen, sixteen, even, some of them were. They were put-out girls, scared runaways most of them. Poor little girls who fought their uncles off but looked tough to us, and mean. God did they look mean. The staff tried to keep them separate from the younger children, but sometimes they caught us watching them in the orchard where they played radios and danced with each other. They'd light out after us and pull our hair or twist our arms. We were scared of them, Roberta and me, but neither of us wanted the other one to know it. So we got a good list of dirty names we could shout back when we ran from them through the orchard. I used to dream a lot and almost always the orchard was there. Two acres, four maybe, of these little apple trees. Hundreds of them. Empty and crooked like beggar women when I first came to St. Bonny's but fat with flowers when I left. I don't know why I dreamt about that orchard so much. Nothing really happened there. Nothing all that important, I mean. Just the big girls dancing and playing the radio. Roberta and me watching. Maggie fell down there once. The kitchen woman with legs like parentheses. And the big girls laughed at her. We should have helped her up, I know, but we were scared of those girls with lipstick and eyebrow pencil. Maggie couldn't talk. The kids said she had her tongue cut out, but I think she was just born that way: mute. She was old and sandy-colored and she worked in the kitchen. I don't know if she was nice or not. I just remember her legs like parentheses and how she rocked when she walked. She worked from early in the morning till two o'clock, and if she was late, if she had too much cleaning and didn't get out till two-fifteen or so, she'd cut through the orchard so she wouldn't miss her bus and have to wait another hour. She wore this really stupid little hat—a kid's hat with ear flaps—and she wasn't much taller than we were. A really awful little hat. Even for a mute, it was dumb—dressing like a kid and never saying anything at all.

"But what about if somebody tries to kill her?" I used to wonder about that. "Or what if she wants to cry? Can she cry?"

"Sure," Roberta said. "But just tears. No sounds come out."

"She can't scream?"

"Nope. Nothing."

"Can she hear?"

"I guess."

"Let's call her," I said. And we did.

"Dummy! Dummy!" She never turned her head.

"Bow legs! Bow legs!" Nothing. She just rocked on, the chin straps of her baby-boy hat swaying from side to side. I think we were wrong. I think she could hear and didn't let on. And it shames me even now to think there was somebody in there after all who heard us call her those names and couldn't tell on us.

We got along all right, Roberta and me. Changed beds every night, got F's in civics and communication skills and gym. The Bozo was disappointed in us, she said. Out of 130 of us state cases, 90 were under twelve. Almost all were real orphans with beautiful dead parents in the sky. We were the only ones dumped and the only ones with F's in three classes including gym. So we got along—what with her leaving whole pieces of things on her plate and being nice about not asking questions.

I think it was the day before Maggie fell down that we found out our mothers were coming to visit us on the same Sunday. We had been at the shelter twenty-eight days (Roberta twenty-eight and a half) and this was their first visit with us. Our mothers would come at ten o'clock in time for chapel, then lunch with us in the teachers' lounge. I thought if my dancing mother met her sick mother it might be good for her. And Roberta thought her sick mother would get a big bang out of a dancing one. We got excited about it and curled each other's hair. After breakfast we sat on the bed watching the road from the window. Roberta's socks were still wet. She washed them the night before and put them on the radiator to dry. They hadn't, but she put them on anyway because their tops were so pretty—scalloped in pink. Each of us had a purple construction-paper basket that we had made in craft class. Mine had a yellow crayon rabbit on it. Roberta's had eggs with wiggly lines of color. Inside were cellophane grass and just the jelly beans because I'd eaten the two marshmallow eggs they gave us. The Big Bozo came herself to get us. Smiling she told us we looked very nice and to come downstairs. We were so surprised by the smile we'd never seen before, neither of us moved.

"Don't you want to see your mommies?"

I stood up first and spilled the jelly beans all over the floor. Bozo's smile disappeared while we scrambled to get the candy up off the floor and put it back in the grass.

She escorted us downstairs to the first floor, where the other girls were lining up to file into the chapel. A bunch of grown-ups stood to one side. Viewers mostly. The old biddies who wanted servants and the fags who wanted company looking for children they might want to adopt. Once in a while a grandmother. Almost never anybody young or anybody whose face wouldn't scare you in the night. Because if any of the real orphans had young relatives they wouldn't be real orphans. I saw Mary right away. She had on those green slacks I hated and hated even more now because didn't she know we were going to chapel? And that fur jacket with the pocket linings so ripped she had to pull to get her hands out of them. But her face was pretty—like always, and she smiled and waved like she was the little girl looking for her mother—not me.

I walked slowly, trying not to drop the jelly beans and hoping the paper handle would hold. I had to use my last Chiclet because by the time I finished cutting everything out, all the Elmer's was gone. I am left-handed and the scissors never worked for me. It didn't matter, though; I might just as well have chewed the gum. Mary dropped to her knees and grabbed me, mashing the basket, the jelly beans, and the grass into her ratty fur jacket.

"Twyla, baby. Twyla, baby!"

I could have killed her. Already I heard the big girls in the orchard the next time saying, "Twyyyyyla, baby!" But I couldn't stay mad at Mary while she was smiling and hugging me and smelling of Lady Esther dusting powder. I wanted to stay buried in her fur all day.

To tell the truth I forgot about Roberta. Mary and I got in line for the traipse into chapel and I was feeling proud because she looked so beautiful even in those ugly green slacks that made her behind stick out. A pretty mother on earth is better than a beautiful dead one in the sky even if she did leave you all alone to go dancing.

I felt a tap on my shoulder, turned, and saw Roberta smiling. I smiled back, but not too much lest somebody think this visit was the biggest thing that ever happened in my life. Then Roberta said, "Mother, I want you to meet my roommate, Twyla. And that's Twyla's mother."

I looked up it seemed for miles. She was big. Bigger than any man and on her chest was the biggest cross I'd ever seen. I swear it was six inches long each way. And in the crook of her arm was the biggest Bible ever made.

Mary, simple-minded as ever, grinned and tried to yank her hand out of the pocket with the raggedy lining—to shake hands, I guess. Roberta's mother looked down at me and then looked down at Mary too. She didn't say anything, just grabbed Roberta with her Bible-free hand and stepped out of line, walking quickly to the rear of it. Mary was still grinning because she's not too swift when it comes to what's really going on. Then this light bulb goes off in her head and she says "That bitch!" really loud and us almost in the chapel now. Organ music whining; the Bonny Angels singing sweetly. Everybody in the world turned around

to look. And Mary would have kept it up—kept calling names
if I hadn't squeezed her hand as hard as I could. That helped a
little, but she still twitched and crossed and uncrossed her legs
all through service. Even groaned a couple of times. Why did I
think she would come there and act right? Slacks. No hat like the
grandmothers and viewers, and groaning all the while. When
we stood for hymns she kept her mouth shut. Wouldn't even look
at the words on the page. She actually reached in her purse for
a mirror to check her lipstick. All I could think of was that she
really needed to be killed. The sermon lasted a year, and I knew
the real orphans were looking smug again.

We were supposed to have lunch in the teachers' lounge, but
Mary didn't bring anything, so we picked fur and cellophane
grass off the mashed jelly beans and ate them. I could have
killed her. I sneaked a look at Roberta. Her mother had brought
chicken legs and ham sandwiches and oranges and a whole box
of chocolate-covered grahams. Roberta drank milk from a ther-
mos while her mother read the Bible to her.

Things are not right. The wrong food is always with the
wrong people. Maybe that's why I got into waitress work later—
to match up the right people with the right food. Roberta just let
those chicken legs sit there, but she did bring a stack of grahams
up to me later when the visit was over. I think she was sorry that
her mother would not shake my mother's hand. And I liked that
and I liked the fact that she didn't say a word about Mary groaning all the way through the service and not bringing any lunch.

Roberta left in May when the apple trees were heavy and
white. On her last day we went to the orchard to watch the big
girls smoke and dance by the radio. It didn't matter that they
said, "Twyyyyyla, baby." We sat on the ground and breathed.

Lady Esther. Apple blossoms. I still go soft when I smell one or the other. Roberta was going home. The big cross and the big Bible was coming to get her and she seemed sort of glad and sort of not. I thought I would die in that room of four beds without her and I knew Bozo had plans to move some other dumped kid in there with me. Roberta promised to write every day, which was really sweet of her because she couldn't read a lick so how could she write anybody. I would have drawn pictures and sent them to her but she never gave me her address. Little by little she faded. Her wet socks with the pink scalloped tops and her big serious-looking eyes—that's all I could catch when I tried to bring her to mind.

I WAS WORKING behind the counter at the Howard Johnson's on the Thruway just before the Kingston exit. Not a bad job. Kind of a long ride from Newburgh, but okay once I got there. Mine was the second night shift—eleven to seven. Very light until a Greyhound checked in for breakfast around six-thirty. At that hour the sun was all the way clear of the hills behind the restaurant. The place looked better at night—more like shelter—but I loved it when the sun broke in, even if it did show all the cracks in the vinyl and the speckled floor looked dirty no matter what the mop boy did.

It was August and a bus crowd was just unloading. They would stand around a long while: going to the john, and looking at gifts and junk-for-sale machines, reluctant to sit down so soon. Even to eat. I was trying to fill the coffee pots and get them all situated on the electric burners when I saw her. She was sitting in a booth smoking a cigarette with two guys smothered in head and facial hair. Her own hair was so big and wild I could hardly see her face. But the eyes. I would know them anywhere. She had on a powder-blue halter and shorts outfit and earrings the size of bracelets. Talk about lipstick and eyebrow pencil. She made the big girls look like nuns. I couldn't get off the counter until seven o'clock, but I kept watching the booth in case they got up to leave before that. My replacement was on time for a change, so I counted and stacked my receipts as fast as I could and signed off. I walked over to the booth, smiling and wondering if she would remember me. Or even if she wanted to remember me. Maybe she didn't want to be reminded of St. Bonny's or to have anybody know she was ever there. I know I never talked about it to anybody.

I put my hands in my apron pockets and leaned against the back of the booth facing them.

"Roberta? Roberta Fisk?"

She looked up. "Yeah?"

"Twyla."

She squinted for a second and then said, "Wow."

"Remember me?"

"Sure. Hey. Wow."

"It's been a while," I said, and gave a smile to the two hairy guys.

"Yeah. Wow. You work here?"

"Yeah," I said. "I live in Newburgh."

"Newburgh? No kidding?" She laughed then a private laugh that included the guys but only the guys, and they laughed with her. What could I do but laugh too and wonder why I was standing there with my knees showing out from under that uniform. Without looking I could see the blue and white triangle on

my head, my hair shapeless in a net, my ankles thick in white
oxfords. Nothing could have been less sheer than my stockings.
There was this silence that came down right after I laughed.
A silence it was her turn to fill up. With introductions, maybe,
to her boyfriends or an invitation to sit down and have a Coke.
Instead she lit a cigarette off the one she'd just finished and said,
"We're on our way to the Coast. He's got an appointment with
Hendrix." She gestured casually toward the boy next to her.

"Hendrix? Fantastic," I said. "Really fantastic. What's she
doing now?"

Roberta coughed on her cigarette and the two guys rolled
their eyes up at the ceiling.

"Hendrix. Jimi Hendrix, asshole. He's only the biggest— Oh,
wow. Forget it."

I was dismissed without anyone saying goodbye, so I thought
I would do it for her.

"How's your mother?" I asked. Her grin cracked her whole
face. She swallowed. "Fine," she said. "How's yours?"

"Pretty as a picture," I said and turned away. The backs of my
knees were damp. Howard Johnson's really was a dump in the
sunlight.

JAMES IS AS COMFORTABLE as a house slipper. He liked my
cooking and I liked his big loud family. They have lived in
Newburgh all of their lives and talk about it the way people do
who have always known a home. His grandmother has a porch
swing older than his father and when they talk about streets
and avenues and buildings they call them names they no longer have. They still call the A & P Rico's because it stands on

property once a mom and pop store owned by Mr. Rico. And
they call the new community college Town Hall because it
once was. My mother-in-law puts up jelly and cucumbers and
buys butter wrapped in cloth from a dairy. James and his father
talk about fishing and baseball and I can see them all together
on the Hudson in a raggedy skiff. Half the population of Newburgh is on welfare now, but to my husband's family it was still
some upstate paradise of a time long past. A time of ice houses
and vegetable wagons, coal furnaces and children weeding gardens. When our son was born my mother-in-law gave me the
crib blanket that had been hers.

But the town they remembered had changed. Something
quick was in the air. Magnificent old houses, so ruined they had
become shelter for squatters and rent risks, were bought and
renovated. Smart IBM people moved out of their suburbs back
into the city and put shutters up and herb gardens in their back-
yards. A brochure came in the mail announcing the opening of
a Food Emporium. Gourmet food it said—and listed items the
rich IBM crowd would want. It was located in a new mall at the
edge of town and I drove out to shop there one day—just to see.
It was late in June. After the tulips were gone and the Queen
Elizabeth roses were open everywhere. I trailed my cart along
the aisle tossing in smoked oysters and Robert's sauce and things
I knew would sit in my cupboard for years. Only when I found
some Klondike ice cream bars did I feel less guilty about spending James's fireman's salary so foolishly. My father-in-law ate
them with the same gusto little Joseph did.

Waiting in the check-out line I heard a voice say, "Twyla!"

The classical music piped over the aisles had affected me and
the woman leaning toward me was dressed to kill. Diamonds

on her hand, a smart white summer dress. "I'm Mrs. Benson,"
I said.

"Ho. Ho. The Big Bozo," she sang.

For a split second I didn't know what she was talking about.
She had a bunch of asparagus and two cartons of fancy water.

"Roberta!"

"Right."

"For heaven's sake. Roberta."

"You look great," she said.

"So do you. Where are you? Here? In Newburgh?"

"Yes. Over in Annandale."

I was opening my mouth to say more when the cashier called
my attention to her empty counter.

"Meet you outside." Roberta pointed her finger and went into
the express line.

I placed the groceries and kept myself from glancing around
to check Roberta's progress. I remembered Howard Johnson's
and looking for a chance to speak only to be greeted with a
stingy "wow." But she was waiting for me and her huge hair was
sleek now, smooth around a small, nicely shaped head. Shoes,
dress, everything lovely and summery and rich. I was dying to
know what happened to her, how she got from Jimi Hendrix to
Annandale, a neighborhood full of doctors and IBM executives.
Easy, I thought. Everything is so easy for them. They think they
own the world.

"How long," I asked her. "How long have you been here?"

"A year. I got married to a man who lives here. And you, you're
married too, right? Benson, you said."

"Yeah. James Benson."

"And is he nice?"

"Oh, is he nice?"

"Well, is he?" Roberta's eyes were steady as though she really meant the question and wanted an answer.

"He's wonderful, Roberta. Wonderful."

"So you're happy."

"Very."

"That's good," she said and nodded her head. "I always hoped you'd be happy. Any kids? I know you have kids."

"One. A boy. How about you?"

"Four."

"Four?"

She laughed. "Step kids. He's a widower."

"Oh."

"Got a minute? Let's have a coffee."

I thought about the Klondikes melting and the inconvenience of going all the way to my car and putting the bags in the trunk. Served me right for buying all that stuff I didn't need. Roberta was ahead of me.

"Put them in my car. It's right here."

And then I saw the dark blue limousine.

"You married a Chinaman?"

"No," she laughed. "He's the driver."

"Oh, my. If the Big Bozo could see you now."

We both giggled. Really giggled. Suddenly, in just a pulse beat, twenty years disappeared and all of it came rushing back. The big girls (whom we called gar girls—Roberta's misheard word for the evil stone faces described in a civics class) there dancing in the orchard, the ploppy mashed potatoes, the double weenies, the Spam with pineapple. We went into the coffee shop holding on to one another and I tried to think why we were glad to see

each other this time and not before. Once, twelve years ago, we
passed like strangers. A black girl and a white girl meeting in a
Howard Johnson's on the road and having nothing to say. One
in a blue and white triangle waitress hat—the other on her way
to see Hendrix. Now we were behaving like sisters separated for
much too long. Those four short months were nothing in time.
Maybe it was the thing itself. Just being there, together. Two
little girls who knew what nobody else in the world knew—how
not to ask questions. How to believe what had to be believed.
There was politeness in that reluctance and generosity as well.
Is your mother sick too? No, she dances all night. Oh—and an
understanding nod.

We sat in a booth by the window and fell into recollection like
veterans.

"Did you ever learn to read?"

"Watch." She picked up the menu. "Special of the day. Cream
of corn soup. Entrées. Two dots and a wriggly line. Quiche. Chef
salad, scallops . . ."

I was laughing and applauding when the waitress came up.

"Remember the Easter baskets?"

"And how we tried to *introduce* them?"

"Your mother with that cross like two telephone poles."

"And yours with those tight slacks."

We laughed so loudly heads turned and made the laughter
harder to suppress.

"What happened to the Jimi Hendrix date?"

Roberta made a blow-out sound with her lips.

"When he died I thought about you."

"Oh, you heard about him finally?"

"Finally. Come on, I was a small-town country waitress."

"And I was a small-town country dropout. God, were we wild. I still don't know how I got out of there alive."

"But you did."

"I did. I really did. Now I'm Mrs. Kenneth Norton."

"Sounds like a mouthful."

"It is."

"Servants and all?"

Roberta held up two fingers.

"Ow! What does he do?"

"Computers and stuff. What do I know?"

"I don't remember a hell of a lot from those days, but Lord, St. Bonny's is as clear as daylight. Remember Maggie? The day she fell down and those gar girls laughed at her?"

Roberta looked up from her salad and stared at me. "Maggie didn't fall," she said.

"Yes, she did. You remember."

"No, Twyla. They knocked her down. Those girls pushed her down and tore her clothes. In the orchard."

"I don't—that's not what happened."

"Sure it is. In the orchard. Remember how scared we were?"

"Wait a minute. I don't remember any of that."

"And Bozo was fired."

"You're crazy. She was there when I left. You left before me."

"I went back. You weren't there when they fired Bozo."

"What?"

"Twice. Once for a year when I was about ten, another for two months when I was fourteen. That's when I ran away."

"You ran away from St. Bonny's?"

"I had to. What do you want? Me dancing in that orchard?"

"Are you sure about Maggie?"

"Of course I'm sure. You've blocked it, Twyla. It happened. Those girls had behavior problems, you know."

"Didn't they, though. But why can't I remember the Maggie thing?"

"Believe me. It happened. And we were there."

"Who did you room with when you went back?" I asked her as if I would know her. The Maggie thing was troubling me.

"Creeps. They tickled themselves in the night."

My ears were itching and I wanted to go home suddenly. This was all very well but she couldn't just comb her hair, wash her face and pretend everything was hunky-dory. After the Howard Johnson's snub. And no apology. Nothing.

"Were you on dope or what that time at Howard Johnson's?" I tried to make my voice sound friendlier than I felt.

"Maybe, a little. I never did drugs much. Why?"

"I don't know; you acted sort of like you didn't want to know me then."

"Oh, Twyla, you know how it was in those days: black—white. You know how everything was."

But I didn't know. I thought it was just the opposite. Busloads of blacks and whites came into Howard Johnson's together. They roamed together then: students, musicians, lovers, protesters. You got to see everything at Howard Johnson's and blacks were very friendly with whites in those days. But sitting there with nothing on my plate but two hard tomato wedges wondering about the melting Klondikes it seemed childish remembering the slight. We went to her car, and with the help of the driver, got my stuff into my station wagon.

"We'll keep in touch this time," she said.

"Sure," I said. "Sure. Give me a call."

"I will," she said, and then just as I was sliding behind the wheel, she leaned into the window. "By the way. Your mother. Did she ever stop dancing?"

I shook my head. "No. Never."

Roberta nodded.

"And yours? Did she ever get well?"

She smiled a tiny sad smile. "No. She never did. Look, call me, okay?"

"Okay," I said, but I knew I wouldn't. Roberta had messed up my past somehow with that business about Maggie. I wouldn't forget a thing like that. Would I?

STRIFE CAME TO US that fall. At least that's what the paper called it. Strife. Racial strife. The word made me think of a bird—a big shrieking bird out of 1,000,000,000 BC. Flapping its wings and cawing. Its eye with no lid always bearing down on you. All day it screeched and at night it slept on the rooftops. It woke you in the morning and from the *Today* show to the eleven o'clock news it kept you an awful company. I couldn't figure it out from one day to the next. I knew I was supposed to feel something strong, but I didn't know what, and James wasn't any help. Joseph was on the list of kids to be transferred from the junior high school to another one at some far-out-of-the-way place and I thought it was a good thing until I heard it was a bad thing. I mean I didn't know. All the schools seemed dumps to me, and the fact that one was nicer looking didn't hold much weight. But the papers were full of it and then the kids began to get jumpy. In August, mind you. Schools weren't even open yet. I thought Joseph might be frightened to go over there, but he didn't seem scared so I forgot about it, until I found myself driving along Hudson Street out there by the school they were trying to integrate and saw a line of women marching. And who do you suppose was in line, big as life, holding a sign in front of her bigger than her mother's cross? MOTHERS HAVE RIGHTS TOO! it said.

I drove on, and then changed my mind. I circled the block, slowed down, and honked my horn.

Roberta looked over and when she saw me she waved. I didn't wave back, but I didn't move either. She handed her sign to another woman and came over to where I was parked.

"Hi."

"What are you doing?"

"Picketing. What's it look like?"

"What for?"

"What do you mean, 'What for?' They want to take my kids and send them out of the neighborhood. They don't want to go."

"So what if they go to another school? My boy's being bussed too, and I don't mind. Why should you?"

"It's not about us, Twyla. Me and you. It's about our kids."

"What's more *us* than that?"

"Well, it is a free country."

"Not yet, but it will be."

"What the hell does that mean? I'm not doing anything to you."

"You really think that?"

"I know it."

"I wonder what made me think you were different."

"I wonder what made me think you were different."

"Look at them," I said. "Just look. Who do they think they are? Swarming all over the place like they own it. And now they think they can decide where my child goes to school. Look at them, Roberta. They're Bozos."

Roberta turned around and looked at the women. Almost all of them were standing still now, waiting. Some were even edging toward us. Roberta looked at me out of some refrigerator behind her eyes. "No, they're not. They're just mothers."

"And what am I? Swiss cheese?"

"I used to curl your hair."

"I hated your hands in my hair."

The women were moving. Our faces looked mean to them of course and they looked as though they could not wait to throw themselves in front of a police car, or better yet, into my car and drag me away by my ankles. Now they surrounded my car and gently, gently began to rock it. I swayed back and forth like a sideways yo-yo. Automatically I reached for Roberta, like the old days in the orchard when they saw us watching them and we had to get out of there, and if one of us fell the other pulled her up and if one of us was caught the other stayed to kick and scratch, and neither would leave the other behind. My arm shot out of the car window but no receiving hand was there. Roberta was look-ing at me sway from side to side in the car and her face was still. My purse slid from the car seat down under the dashboard. The four policemen who had been drinking Tab in their car finally got the message and strolled over, forcing their way through the women. Quietly, firmly they spoke. "Okay, ladies. Back in line or off the streets."

Some of them went away willingly; others had to be urged away from the car doors and the hood. Roberta didn't move. She was looking steadily at me. I was fumbling to turn on the ignition, which wouldn't catch because the gearshift was still in drive. The seats of the car were a mess because the swaying had thrown my grocery coupons all over it and my purse was sprawled on the floor.

"Maybe I am different now, Twyla. But you're not. You're the same little state kid who kicked a poor old black lady when she was down on the ground. You kicked a black lady and you have the nerve to call me a bigot."

The coupons were everywhere and the guts of my purse were bunched under the dashboard. What was she saying? Black? Maggie wasn't black.

"She wasn't black," I said.

"Like hell she wasn't, and you kicked her. We both did. You kicked a black lady who couldn't even scream."

"Liar!"

"You're the liar! Why don't you just go on home and leave us alone, huh?"

She turned away and I skidded away from the curb.

The next morning I went into the garage and cut the side out of the carton our portable TV had come in. It wasn't nearly big enough, but after a while I had a decent sign: red spray-painted letters on a white background—AND SO DO CHIL-DREN****. I meant just to go down to the school and tack it up somewhere so those cows on the picket line across the street could see it, but when I got there, some ten or so others had already assembled—protesting the cows across the street. Police permits and everything. I got in line and we strutted in time on our side while Roberta's group strutted on theirs. That first day we were all dignified, pretending the other side didn't exist. The second day there was name-calling and finger gestures. But that was about all. People changed signs from time to time, but Roberta never did and neither did I. Actually my sign didn't make sense without Roberta's. "And so do children what?" one of the women on my side asked me. Have rights, I said, as though it was obvious.

Roberta didn't acknowledge my presence in any way and I got to thinking maybe she didn't know I was there. I began to pace myself in the line, jostling people one minute and lagging behind the next, so Roberta and I could reach the end of our respective lines at the same time and there would be a moment in our turn when we would face each other. Still, I couldn't tell whether she saw me and knew my sign was for her. The next day I went early before we were scheduled to assemble. I waited until she got there before I exposed my new creation. As soon as she hoisted her MOTHERS HAVE RIGHTS TOO I began to wave my new one, which said, HOW WOULD YOU KNOW? I know she saw that one, but I had gotten addicted now. My signs got crazier each day, and the women on my side decided that I was a kook. They couldn't make heads or tails out of my brilliant screaming posters.

I brought a painted sign in queenly red with huge black letters that said, IS YOUR MOTHER WELL? Roberta took her lunch break and didn't come back for the rest of the day or any day after. Two days later I stopped going too and couldn't have been missed because nobody understood my signs anyway.

It was a nasty six weeks. Classes were suspended and Joseph didn't go to anybody's school until October. The children—everybody's children—soon got bored with that extended vacation they thought was going to be so great. They looked at TV until their eyes flattened. I spent a couple of mornings tutoring my son, as the other mothers said we should. Twice I opened a text from last year that he had never turned in. Twice he yawned in my face. Other mothers organized living room sessions so the kids would keep up. None of the kids could concentrate so they drifted back to *The Price Is Right* and *The Brady Bunch*. When the school finally opened there were fights once or twice and some sirens roared through the streets every once in a while. There were a lot of photographers from Albany. And just when ABC was about to send up a news crew, the kids settled down like nothing in the world had happened. Joseph hung my HOW WOULD YOU KNOW? sign in his bedroom. I don't know what became of AND SO DO CHILDREN****. I think my father-in-law cleaned some fish on it. He was always puttering around in our garage. Each of his five children lived in Newburgh and he acted as though he had five extra homes.

I couldn't help looking for Roberta when Joseph graduated from high school, but I didn't see her. It didn't trouble me much what she had said to me in the car. I mean the kicking part. I know I didn't do that, I couldn't do that. But I was puzzled by her telling me Maggie was black. When I thought about it I actually couldn't be certain. She wasn't pitch-black, I knew, or I would have remembered that. What I remember was the kiddie hat, and the semicircle legs. I tried to reassure myself about the race thing for a long time until it dawned on me that the truth was already there, and Roberta knew it. I didn't kick her; I didn't join in with the gar girls and kick that lady, but I sure did want to. We watched and never tried to help her and never called for help. Maggie was my dancing mother. Deaf, I thought, and dumb. Nobody inside. Nobody who would hear you if you cried in the night. Nobody who could tell you anything important that you could use. Rocking, dancing, swaying as she walked. And when the gar girls pushed her down, and started roughhousing, I knew she wouldn't scream, couldn't—just like me—and I was glad about that.

WE DECIDED NOT to have a tree, because Christmas would be at my mother-in-law's house, so why have a tree at both places? Joseph was at SUNY New Paltz and we had to economize, we said. But at the last minute, I changed my mind. Nothing could be that bad. So I rushed around town looking for a tree, something small but wide. By the time I found a place, it was snowing and very late. I dawdled like it was the most important purchase in the world and the tree man was fed up with me. Finally I chose one and had it tied onto the trunk of the car. I drove away slowly because the sand trucks were not out yet and the streets could be murder at the beginning of a snowfall. Downtown the streets were wide and rather empty except for a cluster of people coming out of the Newburgh Hotel. The one hotel in town that wasn't built out of cardboard and Plexiglas. A party, probably. The men huddled in the snow were dressed in tails and the women had on furs. Shiny things glittered from underneath their coats. It made me tired to look at them. Tired, tired, tired. On the next corner was a small diner with loops and loops of paper bells in the window. I stopped the car and went in. Just for a cup of coffee and twenty minutes of peace before I went home and tried to finish everything before Christmas Eve.

"Twyla?"

There she was. In a silvery evening gown and dark fur coat. A man and another woman were with her, the man fumbling for change to put in the cigarette machine. The woman was humming and tapping on the counter with her fingernails. They all looked a little bit drunk.

"Well. It's you."

"How are you?"

I shrugged. "Pretty good. Frazzled. Christmas and all."

"Regular?" called the woman from the counter.

"Fine," Roberta called back and then, "Wait for me in the car."

She slipped into the booth beside me. "I have to tell you something, Twyla. I made up my mind if I ever saw you again, I'd tell you."

"I'd just as soon not hear anything, Roberta. It doesn't matter now, anyway."

"No," she said. "Not about that."

"Don't be long," said the woman. She carried two regulars to go and the man peeled his cigarette pack as they left.

"It's about St. Bonny's and Maggie."

"Oh, please."

"Listen to me. I really did think she was black. I didn't make that up. I really thought so. But now I can't be sure. I just remember her as old, so old. And because she couldn't talk—well, you know, I thought she was crazy. She'd been brought up in an institution like my mother was and like I thought I would be too. And you were right. We didn't kick her. It was the gar girls. Only them. But, well, I wanted to. I really wanted them to hurt her. I said we did it, too. You and me, but that's not true. And I don't want you to carry that around. It was just that I wanted to do it so bad that day—wanting to is doing it."

Her eyes were watery from the drinks she'd had, I guess. I

know it's that way with me. One glass of wine and I start bawling over the littlest thing.

"We were kids, Roberta."

"Yeah. Yeah. I know, just kids."

"Eight."

"Eight."

"And lonely."

"Scared, too."

She wiped her cheeks with the heel of her hand and smiled. "Well, that's all I wanted to say."

I nodded and couldn't think of any way to fill the silence that went from the diner past the paper bells on out into the snow. It was heavy now. I thought I'd better wait for the sand trucks before starting home.

"Thanks, Roberta."

"Sure."

"Did I tell you? My mother, she never did stop dancing."

"Yes. You told me. And mine, she never got well." Roberta lifted her hands from the tabletop and covered her face with her palms. When she took them away she really was crying. "Oh shit, Twyla. Shit, shit, shit. What the hell happened to Maggie?"

DISCUSSION QUESTIONS

1. How does Morrison play with race in this story?

2. How did your interpretations of Twyla and Roberta change as the story progressed?

3. Twyla recalls her friendship with Roberta with nostalgia: "Two little girls who knew what nobody else in the world knew—how not

to ask questions. How to believe what had to be believed." Later, as women, they say to each other: "I wonder what made me think you were different." How much does telling the truth or obscuring it play a part in the functionality of their relationship?

4. Why do you think Morrison named this short story "Recitatif"?

The Richer, the Poorer

Dorothy West

Originally published in 1995

At our time of life, it's the days that count. You've too much catching up to do to waste a minute of a waking hour feeling sorry for yourself.

Over the years Lottie had urged Bess to prepare for her old age. Over the years Bess had lived each day as if there were no other. Now they were both past sixty, the time for summing up. Lottie had a bank account that had never grown lean. Bess had the clothes on her back, and the rest of her worldly possessions in a battered suitcase.

Lottie had hated being a child, hearing her parents' skimping and scraping. Bess had never seemed to notice. All she ever wanted was to go outside and play. She learned to skate on borrowed skates. She rode a borrowed bicycle. Lottie couldn't wait to grow up and buy herself the best of everything.

As soon as anyone would hire her, Lottie put herself to work. She minded babies, she ran errands for the old.

She never touched a penny of her money, though her child's

mouth watered for ice cream and candy. But she could not bear to share with Bess, who never had anything to share with her. When the dimes began to add up to dollars, she lost her taste for sweets.

By the time she was twelve, she was clerking after school in a small variety store. Saturdays she worked as long as she was wanted. She decided to keep her money for clothes. When she entered high school, she would wear a wardrobe that neither she nor anyone else would be able to match.

But her freshman year found her unable to indulge so frivolous a whim, particularly when her admiring instructors advised her to think seriously of college. No one in her family had ever gone to college, and certainly Bess would never get there. She would show them all what she could do, if she put her mind to it.

She began to bank her money, and her bankbook became her most private and precious possession.

In her third year of high school she found a job in a small but expanding restaurant, where she cashiered from the busy hour until closing. In her last year of high school the business increased so rapidly that Lottie was faced with the choice of staying in school or working full time.

She made her choice easily. A job in hand was worth two in the future.

Bess had a beau in the school band, who had no other ambition except to play a horn. Lottie expected to be settled with a home and family while Bess was still waiting for Harry to earn enough to buy a marriage license.

That Bess married Harry straight out of high school was not surprising. That Lottie never married at all was not really

surprising either. Two or three times she was halfway persuaded, but to give up a job that paid well for a homemaking job
that paid nothing was a risk she was incapable of taking.

Bess's married life was nothing for Lottie to envy. She and
Harry lived like gypsies, Harry playing in second-rate bands
all over the country, even getting himself and Bess stranded in
Europe. They were often in rags and never in riches.

Bess grieved because she had no child, not having sense
enough to know she was better off without one. Lottie was certainly better off without nieces and nephews to feel sorry for.
Very likely Bess would have dumped them on her doorstep.

That Lottie had a doorstep they might have been left on was
only because her boss, having bought a second house, offered
Lottie his first house at a price so low and terms so reasonable
that it would have been like losing money to refuse.

She shut off the rooms she didn't use, letting them go to rack
and ruin. Since she ate her meals out, she had no food at home,
and did not encourage callers, who always expected a cup of tea.

Her way of life was mean and miserly, but she did not know
it. She thought she lived frugally in her middle years so that
she could live in comfort and ease when she most needed peace
of mind.

The years, after forty, began to race. Suddenly Lottie was
sixty, and retired from her job by her boss's son, who had no sen-
timental feeling about keeping her on until she was ready to quit.

She made several attempts to find other employment, but her
dowdy appearance made her look old and inefficient. For the first
time in her life Lottie would gladly have worked for nothing, to
have some place to go, something to do with her day.

Harry died abroad, in a third-rate hotel, with Bess weeping as hard as if he had left her a fortune. He had left her nothing but his horn. There wasn't even money for her passage home.

Lottie, trapped by the blood tie, knew she would not only have to send for her sister, but take her in when she returned. It didn't seem fair that Bess should reap the harvest of Lottie's lifetime of self-denial.

It took Lottie a week to get a bedroom ready, a week of hard work and hard cash. There was everything to do, everything to replace or paint. When she was through the room looked so fresh and new that Lottie felt she deserved it more than Bess.

She would let Bess have her room, but the mattress was so lumpy, the carpet so worn, the curtains so threadbare that Lottie's conscience pricked her. She supposed she would have to redo that room, too, and went about doing it with an eagerness that she mistook for haste.

When she was through upstairs, she was shocked to see how dismal downstairs looked by comparison. She tried to ignore it, but with nowhere to go to escape it, the contrast grew more intolerable.

She worked her way from kitchen to parlor, persuading herself she was only putting the rooms to rights to give herself something to do. At night she slept like a child after a long and happy day of playing house. She was having more fun than she had ever had in her life. She was living each hour for itself.

There was only a day now before Bess would arrive. Passing her gleaming mirrors, at first with vague awareness, then with painful clarity, Lottie saw herself as others saw her, and could not stand the sight.

She went on a spending spree from the specialty shops to

beauty salon, emerging transformed into a woman who believed
in miracles.

She was in the kitchen basting a turkey when Bess rang the
bell. Her heart raced, and she wondered if the heat from the oven
was responsible.

She went to the door, and Bess stood before her. Stiffly she suffered Bess's embrace, her heart racing harder, her eyes suddenly
smarting from the onrush of cold air.

"Oh, Lottie, it's good to see you," Bess said, but saying nothing
about Lottie's splendid appearance. Upstairs Bess, putting down
her shabby suitcase, said, "I'll sleep like a rock tonight," without a word of praise for her lovely room. At the lavish table, top-
heavy with turkey, Bess said, "I'll take light and dark, both," with
no marveling at the size of the bird, or that there was turkey for
two elderly women, one of them too poor to buy her own bread.

With the glow of good food in her stomach, Bess began to spin
stories. They were rich with places and people, most of them
lowly, all of them magnificent. Her face reflected her telling, the
joys and sorrows of her remembering, and above all, the love she
lived by that enhanced the poorest place, the humblest person.

Then it was that Lottie knew why Bess had made no mention of her finery, or the shining room, or the twelve-pound turkey. She had not even seen them. Tomorrow she would see the
room as it really looked, and Lottie as she really looked, and the
warmed-over turkey in its second-day glory. Tonight she saw
only what she had come seeking, a place in her sister's home
and heart.

She said, "That's enough about me. How have the years used
you?"

"It was me who didn't use them," said Lottie wistfully. "I

saved for them. I saved for them. I forgot the best of them would go without my ever spending a day or a dollar enjoying them. That's my life story in those few words, a life never lived.

"Now it's too near the end to try."

Bess said, "To know how much there is to know is the beginning of learning to live. Don't count the years that are left us. At our time of life it's the days that count. You've too much catching up to do to waste a minute of a waking hour feeling sorry for yourself."

Lottie grinned, a real wide-open grin, "Well to tell the truth, I felt sorry for you. Maybe if I had any sense I'd feel sorry for myself, after all. I know I'm too old to kick up my heels, but I'm going to let you show me how. If I land on my head, I guess it won't matter; I feel giddy already, and I like it."

DISCUSSION QUESTIONS

1. While the characters in this story are adults, there is imagery of girlhood laced throughout: "She worked her way from kitchen to parlor, persuading herself she was only putting the rooms to rights to give herself something to do. At night she slept like a child after a long and happy day of playing house." What does this convey? How do their distinct life choices contribute to the emotional impact of the narrative?

2. Compare and contrast the sisters' identities. What do they want out of life? How does this trace back to childhood ambitions? Which sister is more innocent?

Fifth Sunday

Rita Dove

Originally published in 1985

Only when she daydreamed did Valerie experience
the power of hope, a sense of luxurious apprehension.

The church stood on a hill all to itself, at the intersec-
tion of Prospect and Maple. Opposite the broad, shal-
low steps and the three sets of double doors was a small
ash-and-gravel parking lot, room for only a handful of cars; the
minister and his assistants had reserved spaces, while the rest
of the congregation used the side streets. Valerie's father always
parked parallel to Prospect, nosing the sleek car down the steep
brick road lined by abandoned houses and devil-strips over-
grown to knee-level, weeds topped by sinister furred knobs.

Catercorner from the church was a park. It was everything a
park should be: green, shaded, quiet. Stout black poles marked
its perimeter at regular intervals, and strung between each pole
were two chains, one at waist-level and another six inches from
the ground. The park itself was segmented by two concrete

paths that cut it on the diagonals, like a huge envelope. The paths seemed to serve no other purpose than help people walk through the park as quickly as possible: there were no animals, no vendors, no bandstand; Valerie could not remember ever seeing anyone sitting on the few chilly benches.

Valerie and the other young people of the church used the park as a shortcut to the all-night coffeehouse on East Exchange Street. "Max's Diner" was connected to a motel; each Sunday morning an exciting, bedraggled assortment of people could be found at the L-shaped counter. The waitress was called Vera; her upswept blonde hair resembled a fanciful antique urn. She was friendly; sometimes she even let them sit at the counter.

Usually they didn't have time to take a seat. Main Service began at eleven sharp; and though Sunday School was supposed to be over at 10:30, often their teacher, Mr. Brown, got so carried away that they had to resort to coughs and exaggerated glances at the clock before he caught on and let them loose—but not before a five-minute lecture on obedience and diligence that made it nearly eleven by the time they got to Max's. . . .

Of course, it hadn't always been like that. When she was little, Valerie wouldn't have dared slip off to any place as worldly as a diner. But now that she had been promoted to the Upper Sunday School, it was a matter of course to have a Mounds bar for furtive munching during church. The park hadn't always been a thoroughfare, either. Many, many years ago Valerie's mother had first been kissed there. She had been in the junior choir, and there was a boy among the tenors named John, with light brown eyes and long dark lashes. Choir rehearsals were on Tuesday evenings; before rehearsals the two of them, Valerie's mother and John, had taken to walking in the park. It was summer; the birds sat as if drugged in the trees. He touched her hand and then her cheek, and then he kissed her.

What was it like? "Nice—a kiss," was all her mother had to say about it. Valerie was fourteen and had never been kissed. It was impossible to imagine it ever happening. How did one go about it? Sure, there were plenty of boys around who wanted to—loud boys with scabs on their knuckles. No, she would have to like a boy before she let him kiss her. But as soon as she started to like someone, she got shy and tongue-tied whenever he tried to talk to her. What other choice did he have but to lose interest? No one can like a stone.

Church was the most glorious part of her existence. Her schoolmates she saw every day, in the halls or around the neighborhood—but when Sunday came, she would put on her best clothes and ride to the other side of the city. Deep familial traditions gave the church a varied congregation—people from all parts of town and all social and economic levels filled the dark waxed pews, so that once a week Valerie had friends who were different and met boys who played basketball in rival high schools. No wonder she scorned her classmates and looked forward to Sunday as if to a party.

She was not in the choir but in the junior ushers. Ever since she could remember, Valerie knew she would join one or the other. Whenever the choir stood up, their blue silk robes swaying slightly as they rocked to the beat, an amorphous yearning would surge in her, crystallizing to a single thought: *I can sing!* she would whisper, and bite her lip. Everyone knew, though, that most of the girls in the junior choir were "fast"; nowadays it was no honor to be associated with it.

Andrew was another reason for joining the usher board. He

was the president. He was also the minister's son, and as such the undisputed leader of the male youth. He was very ugly—a pasty yellow color, and he wore his sandy hair in a short squarish afro, since it was too kinky to wear fuller. An overlarge lower lip pulled his mouth open slightly, exposing a row of widely spaced teeth. His ears stood out and the lobes were covered with tiny indentations, as if someone had pricked them with a fork, like a pie shell. And he was blind in one eye. The story went that when he was ten he had been in a snowball fight; somebody threw a snowball with a stone in it. Valerie had to catch her breath whenever she thought of it. Imagine—you're playing outside with no other thought but fun when suddenly, from nowhere, a hard coldness slams into you—an arrow of ice—and when it's all over, you've lost half your sight. It must be horrible. It must be something you could never forget. Valerie found herself staring at Andrew. Of a mottled gray-blue color, both eyes were so beautifully vague that when the light struck them they seemed to disappear. If she watched closely she could pick up the slightly slower reaction of one iris, the minute flagging of the right eyelid when he looked sideways.

It endears him to me, Valerie said silently to herself as they drove home from church. After the car had crunched through the gravel driveway and she was safely in her room and had slipped off her patent-leather T-straps, she looked earnestly into the mirror and said, aloud this time: *It endears him to me.* She studied the tiny pearl earrings her parents had given her for graduation from grade school; she took them off, unscrewing the silver fastenings and locking them in the padded jewelry box. Andrew was seventeen. She had no chance.

She clutched to her passion like a pillow or a torch. On long

Saturday afternoons she dreamed about the kiss to come—there was the park, there were the smoke-and-sky eyes to replace the light brown ones. Only when she daydreamed did Valerie experience the power of hope, a sense of luxurious apprehension.

One Saturday night the young people of the white Lutheran church one block over invited the black youth to see a movie on Martin Luther King. Valerie's mother dropped her off. It was still a little early, so she walked over to Prospect and stood for a while on the corner, looking down the hill.

This was not the choked, winding alley where her father parked—here the road fell straight and sharply into the city below. And she was on top of it, looking down. She really didn't know why she had walked to the church—maybe on the chance that the minister was inside working, and that Andrew might come walking out—maybe. But as she stood there looking down at the flushed sky and the indistinct trees clumped below it and below them, the tiny gray houses in the tiny gray streets, she felt a glow inside her chest—like a net with a brilliant fish struggling to escape—and she felt strong. Even the cool white steps of the church were not her equal.

She went back to the Lutheran church, where everyone had gathered in the basement. There were introductions, then the announcement for the start of the movie. Valerie was about to sit next to the aisle when Andrew came up and asked if she minded him sitting next to her. "Of course not," she said, and broke into a sweat behind her knees. She scooted over, trying to regain her composure. But Andrew would not wait for that. He plied her with questions—what kind of music did she like? Was she going to the high school track meet next week? He was sitting to her right, so the good eye could see every movement she made—still, whenever he said something, he turned so that they were face-to-face, the unresponsive eye giving him a vulnerable look. Then the lights went out. He crossed his legs and leaned back, throwing his left arm across the back of her chair; terrified, Valerie sat very still and tried to concentrate on the movie. From time to time Andrew would take away his arm, lean forward, and whisper in her ear; his comments were so hilarious that she could hardly keep from laughing out loud, and before the film was over she even managed a few witticisms of her own.

The next day was Fifth Sunday. Whenever there was a fifth Sunday in a month, the young people presided over the main service. They ushered, provided music, read the text from the Scriptures, passed the collection plate—even led the congregation in prayer for the sick and shut-in. The only thing they did not do was give the sermon. Valerie was so excited from the previous evening that she barely ate anything at breakfast. She had slept very little; and at seven she finally got up to press the knife-pleated white skirt. She hated their uniforms. The skirt was made from some synthetic material that stuck to her legs; the baggy white blouse was not cool at all. Besides, her period had started, which meant that she would have to wear the plastic-lined panties that made her feel like a baby in diapers.

Today, however, even that could not discourage her. Andrew would forgo ushering to help at the altar, so today she could look at him as much as she pleased.

It was a hot, humid morning, and by 10:30 everyone looked limp and disgruntled. As on every Sunday when they ushered, the junior ushers did not go to Max's but convened in the small lounge off the main lobby. The decision who was going to "key" had to be made, and it was always a controversial one. There were four aisles to be covered. The side aisles had the least traffic and the windows. The right middle aisle was called the "key." Most of the people came down this aisle. The old, respected members had their regular seats in the front pews; the choir marched down this aisle and up into the chancel; all the fashionable middle class who'd come to show off their new clothes wanted seats in the middle section where they could be seen. The key usher had to remember where the regulars sat, get out of the way of the choir, gesture grandly to the bourgeoise's chosen pew, and take messages to the pulpit. Nobody wanted to be key.

Valerie was assigned aisle three. Of course she was glad she didn't have to key. But almost as many people came down her aisle as down the other middle aisle. It was strange how people always streamed toward the middle of any place. At the supermarket they fought for a parking space in the thick of all the other cars; after church in the lobby or on the steps they gravitated toward the largest groups, squeezing through the outer fringe to get a better angle on the discussion in the inner circle. But at least—even if she didn't have a window—she had an unobstructed view of the altar. Except when the congregation stood up to sing, she could see Andrew clearly. He wore a light blue suit with a yellow shirt just a shade brighter than his skin. He looked self-confident, compassionate. He caught her glance and smiled.

The doors opened and people poured in. Valerie was shy of them. They were always in a hurry to be seated and never really looked at her. Today, though, she felt she was getting through it fairly well—although once when there was a crush of people, she had trouble with an old man whose cane kept getting jammed between the pews and some woman in a pink silk hat squeezed past Valerie impatiently, the thick scent of her perfume trailing

her like fame itself. Valerie's stomach was growling; she hoped
no one could hear it.

Sunlight bowled through the vaulted windows; sweat stood
out in delicate beaded patterns on the powdered brows of the
women; the cardboard fans in the hands of the junior choir
members flitted at an amazing rate, like small scared birds. Valerie felt the dampness under her arms, between her shoulder
blades, inside the plastic pants. Her stockings felt like they had
been dragged in wet sand—in fact she itched all over, and she
kept shifting her weight from one foot to the other and adjusting her white gloves. *I'll stick it out until this song is over and then
I'll leave the floor*, she thought; but when the congregation had
regained their seats Valerie felt that would look too conspicu-
ous; so she decided to wait until the responsive reading was
over. She tried concentrating on a sunbeam that bisected the
small table where the gleaners were arrayed. *After the responsive reading*, she thought, *the little girls in their white robes will
march up to the altar, and each one will take a gleaner and pass it
from row to row, and each person will take out a dime or a nickel
and drop it in the slot* ... Valerie thought of the sound all those
coins clinking against glass would make. The sunbeam had separated into tiny glowing dots, and there were particles of dust
suspended between the spots—the sun glancing off of all that silver made her dizzy. . . .

How cool it had become suddenly, and a breeze too! It was
a relief to be able to take her mind off her problems. At any
rate, she was glad the weather had broken. Now she was lying
in a hammock on the back porch with a tall cool glass of punch
beside her. As she rocked back and forth, the wind—no, no more
than a breath, a zephyr!—lifted her hair to dry her forehead, then

dropped each strand gently back into place. Far away the door-bell rang. She heard her mother's voice, then footsteps growing louder and the screen door slamming; she swooned in delicious anticipation, and then Andrew was beside her with a cool hand for her forehead and a gaze of tender solicitude radiating from the watery depths of his eyes. . . .

Why did she feel so terrible all of a sudden, and why had the sun come back? For a moment there was nothing but a piercing whiteness, and Valerie felt as if she were floating—but badly, in jerks and bobs. Someone was whispering below her . . . what were they saying? *She must have fainted.*

No! Valerie tried to lift her head but only succeeded in look-ing down the length of her own body, which was stiff as a board. Several men were carrying her down the aisle. The service had stopped; she lifted her head again, and this time saw the choir's and the minister's startled faces suspended at the far end of the aisle. Then they were gone.

She was laid out on a couch in the lounge and a fat woman in white with a businesslike manner stuck something under her nose. An electric shock jolted her to the base of her spine. After the coolness and the dream of Andrew, this nausea! She felt wounded in her soul. More than anything she was ashamed.

Faces mooned above her and hands undid her collar, rubbed her wrists. None of their administrations did anything but agi-tate her still further, and she was about to tell them so (if she could only get her mouth to cooperate), when a woman Valerie did not recognize appeared at the foot of the couch and leaned over her. The woman made no attempt to help; she looked Val-erie up and down with a hard cool stare and said, "Who knows? Maybe she's pregnant."

Valerie sputtered, struggling onto her elbows, but the nurse held her down. "It's not true!" she gasped and tried to get up again. The circle of faces closed in on her, whispering soothing things she could not understand. The woman had disappeared. No one would tell Valerie her name, though she thrashed and pleaded.

Valerie's parents had arrived. Her father stood awkwardly to one side as her mother knelt beside the couch and looked at her with large, troubled eyes. Valerie barely noticed them; she was thinking of the woman spitting that word over her like a pronouncement: *pregnant*. Well, the bitch wouldn't get away with it. There weren't that many people in this church she didn't know— she'd find out who she was. She'd make them tell. Bitch. She'd find her. She'd find her.

DISCUSSION QUESTIONS

1. The church plays a prominent role in Valerie's life: "Church was the most glorious part of her existence." How does Dove use this setting to deepen the story?

2. Throughout the story, Valerie develops her self-worth and sense of community at church. What unique experiences shape her understanding of the individual people that make up the congregation?

3. How do you interpret the ending of the story? Why does Valerie faint? And what does her response to fainting tell us?

4. What do you see for Valerie in the coming years? Do you believe she will grow more self-confident or vindictive?

Belonging

Who We Are

Camille Acker

Originally published in 2018

We laugh and curse and scream. The people in suits and ties and nice dresses and heels give us looks. Until. They turn to look out the window. Or look down into their *Washington Post*s. We talk louder to make them look.

We walk down the halls like we are coming to beat you up. Even the teachers move out of the way. No one wants to catch an elbow in their ribs or a foot in their stride. They look away when we pass. Or take a turn down a hallway where we are not. We will make them into a joke anyway. Something about their face. Or their clothes. Or their name. We decide who they are.

When we go to lunch, we take up three tables. We need only two. Nobody will ask us to move. We sign up for the same classes. The easy ones. The white kids want the advanced placement classes. They make you take tests to get into them. Tests we never have liked. We don't like teachers either. They tell us what to do. We don't let anybody tell us what to do.

We cut class. Almost every day. The security guards are black like us so we just dap them up. Then, we go. When we leave, we go to the movies down the street. Pay for one. And then go theater to theater seeing all the shows we want.

We eat. At McDonald's. Or the Chinese takeout. Or sometimes we go to nicer places where they give you real menus. We sit there eating and laughing. The owners say we should quiet down. We decide that to teach them, we won't pay. And we run out on the bill. Sometimes even when they don't say something, we run out on the bill.

And then we stroll all around Upper Northwest. We walk past real nice houses with real nice cars. Only one car in the driveway. The other one gone. Probably in some garage at the State Department. Or on the Hill. Or Downtown at one of the law firms. Every house has a big porch and around Christmas they have lights wound around the columns. A lit-up plastic snowman. A wreath on the door. And at Halloween, the houses have a skeleton and cotton made to look like cobwebs. A cackling witch.

We go to school with some of their kids. Or their kids go to Sidwell. Or Holton-Arms. Or Georgetown Day. Their kids take classes at colleges too. A couple of days a week at American or GW. They come home and tell their parents about how the Germans get talked about more for what they did in World War II, but some people think the Japanese were worse. We don't tell our parents things like that. We pretend we don't even know things like that.

We go to this field with this old, abandoned stage. We sit there because we don't sit in grass like white people. We sit on the warped old wood. It cracks and we crack on each other. And sometimes we make out. And sometimes we act like having someone else's tongue in our mouth is nice. Or that having hands on our body is good. When we get to underwear, we stop there so we don't get embarrassed.

And some days there is alcohol from a cousin who says not to tell our parents, and some days there is alcohol from way back in the cabinet on the lower right side of our parents' stash. Once or twice, there is weed. And we lie on the stage, venturing splinters, surrounded by each other, not looking anybody in the face. And we feel lots of things we can't say. Until we hit each other or pull each other's hair and go back to pretending we don't feel anything at all.

When we leave for the day, we get on the Metro. We swing around the poles. And lean over the people sitting in priority seating and act like we're looking at the map. We laugh and curse and scream. The people in suits and ties and nice dresses and heels give us looks. Until. They turn to look out the window. Or look down into their *Washington Post*s. We talk louder to make them look. And we don't stop until we see that they're afraid. That they walk way down to the other end of the subway car to exit through that door instead of the door near us.

We always see an old lady on the train. Not the same one, but one tough enough to not look away. We won't notice at first that she sees us. Then, when we do, we call her out on it.

"Excuse me, ma'am?" we say. "I'm sorry to bother you, ma'am."

"Yes?" she answers and smiles.

"Well, ma'am, I wanted to ask you a question. If it's not too much trouble," we say with our serious face.

"Go ahead," she says. Encouraging us. Discouraging her fears.

We smile at her. "My friend wants to know if you'd suck his dick," we say. We laugh big. With our faces. With our bodies. We fall into each other. We fall over the seats.

She moves as far away from us as she can. We have her surrounded. She is trapped in her seat. She pushes against the window as if she could escape. Get out of the train. Tumble onto the tracks. We calm down. Only for the rest of the ride, we call out to her, "Ma'am? Excuse me, ma'am?" so we can laugh some more. When we get off, we can see that the old lady is still scared. That she hates us because we are everything she has tried to deny that we are. We are everything she has thought but has never said.

We have shown her.

DISCUSSION QUESTIONS

1. There is no "I" in this story—Acker uses the first person "we." How would a different point of view have changed the story?

2. Does the short story offer the reader insight into the lives, dreams, and hardships of those young students described? What is the tone? What does it tell you about belonging?

3. We observe how the students collectively engage with adults and navigate their surroundings. Do you think their friendships are ultimately strengthened or weakened by the choices they make?

4. Can you think of a time when you were a "we" in a group? Did you feel empowered by it?

The Lesson

Toni Cade Bambara

Originally published in 1972

So we heading down the street and she's boring us silly about what things cost and what our parents make and how much goes for rent and how money ain't divided up right in this country.

Back in the days when everyone was old and stupid or young and foolish and me and Sugar were the only ones just right, this lady moved on our block with nappy hair and proper speech and no makeup. And quite naturally we laughed at her, laughed the way we did at the junk man who went about his business like he was some big-time president and his sorry-ass horse his secretary. And we kinda hated her too, hated the way we did the winos who cluttered up our parks and pissed on our handball walls and stank up our hallways and stairs so you couldn't halfway play hide-and-seek without a goddamn gas mask. Miss Moore was her name. The only woman on the block with no first name. And she was black as hell, cept for her feet, which were fish-white and spooky. And she was always planning these boring-ass things for us to do, us being my cousin, mostly, who lived on the block cause we all moved North the same time and to the same apartment then spread out gradual to breathe. And our parents would yank our heads into some kinda shape and crisp up our clothes so we'd be presentable for travel with Miss Moore, who always looked like she was going to church though she never did. Which is just one of the things the grown-ups talked about when they talked behind her back like a dog. But when she came calling with some sachet she'd sewed up or some gingerbread she'd made or some book, why then they'd all be too embarrassed to turn her down and we'd get handed over all spruced up. She'd been to college and said it was only right that she should take responsibility for the young ones' education, and she not even related by marriage or blood. So they'd go for it. Specially Aunt Gretchen. She was the main gofer in the family. You got some ole dumb shit foolishness you want somebody to go for, you send for Aunt Gretchen. She been screwed into the go-along for so long, it's a blood-deep natural thing with her. Which is how she got saddled with me and Sugar and Junior in the first place while our mothers were in a la-de-da apartment up the block having a good ole time.

So this one day Miss Moore rounds us all up at the mailbox and it's puredee hot and she's knockin herself out about arith-metic. And school suppose to let up in summer I heard, but she don't never let up. And the starch in my pinafore scratching the shit outta me and I'm really hating this nappy-head bitch and her goddamn college degree. I'd much rather go to the pool or to the show where it's cool. So me and Sugar leaning on the mail-box being surly, which is a Miss Moore word. And Flyboy check-ing out what everybody brought for lunch. And Fat Butt already wasting his peanut-butter-and-jelly sandwich like the pig he is. And Junebug punchin on Q.T.'s arm for potato chips. And Rosie Giraffe shifting from one hip to the other waiting for somebody to step on her foot or ask her if she from Georgia so she can kick ass, preferably Mercedes'. And Miss Moore asking us do we know what money is like we a bunch of retards. I mean real money, she say, like it's only poker chips or monopoly papers we lay on the grocer. So right away I'm tired of this and say so. And would much rather snatch Sugar and go to the Sunset and terrorize the West Indian kids and take their hair ribbons and their money too. And Miss Moore files that remark away for next week's lesson on brotherhood, I can tell. And finally I say we oughta get to the subway cause it's cooler an' besides we might meet some cute boys. Sugar done swiped her mama's lipstick, so we ready.

So we heading down the street and she's boring us silly about what things cost and what our parents make and how much goes for rent and how money ain't divided up right in this country. And then she gets to the part about we all poor and live in the slums which I don't feature. And I'm ready to speak on that, but she steps out in the street and hails two cabs just like that. Then she hustles half the crew in with her and hands me a five-dollar bill and tells me to calculate 10 percent tip for the driver. And we're off. Me and Sugar and Junebug and Flyboy hangin out the window and hollering to everybody, putting lipstick on each other cause Flyboy a faggot anyway, and making farts with our sweaty armpits. But I'm mostly trying to figure how to spend this money. But they are fascinated with the meter ticking and Junebug starts laying bets as to how much it'll read when Flyboy can't hold his breath no more. Then Sugar lays bets as to how much it'll be when we get there. So I'm stuck. Don't nobody want to go for my plan, which is to jump out at the next light and run off to the first bar-b-que we can find. Then the driver tells us to get the hell out cause we there already. And the meter reads eighty-five cents. And I'm stalling to figure out the tip and Sugar say give him a dime. And I decide he don't need it bad as I do, so later for him. But then he tries to take off with Junebug foot still in the door so we talk about his mama something ferocious. Then we check out that we on Fifth Avenue and everybody dressed up in stockings. One lady in a fur coat, hot as it is. White folks crazy.

"This is the place," Miss Moore say, presenting it to us in the voice she uses at the museum. "Let's look in the windows before we go in."

"Can we steal?" Sugar asks very serious like she's getting the ground rules squared away before she plays. "I beg your pardon," say Miss Moore, and we fall out. So she leads us around the windows of the toy store and me and Sugar screamin, "This is mine, that's mine, I gotta have that, that was made for me, I was born for that," till Big Butt drowns us out.

"Hey, I'm goin to buy that there."

"That there? You don't even know what it is, stupid."

"I do so," he say punchin on Rosie Giraffe. "It's a microscope."

"Whatcha gonna do with a microscope, fool?"

"Look at things."

"Like what, Ronald?" ask Miss Moore. And Big Butt ain't got the first notion. So here go Miss Moore gabbing about the thousands of bacteria in a drop of water and the somethinorother in a speck of blood and the million and one living things in the air around us is invisible to the naked eye. And what she say that for? Junebug go to town on that "naked" and we rolling. Then Miss Moore ask what it cost. So we all jam into the window smudgin it up and the price tag say $300. So then she ask how long'd take for Big Butt and Junebug to save up their allowances. "Too long," I say. "Yeh," adds Sugar, "outgrown it by that time." And Miss Moore say no, you never outgrow learning instruments. "Why, even medical students and interns and," blah, blah, blah. And we ready to choke Big Butt for bringing it up in the first damn place.

"This here costs four hundred eighty dollars," say Rosie Giraffe. So we pile up all over her to see what she pointin out. My eyes tell me it's a chunk of glass cracked with something heavy, and different-color inks dripped into the splits, then the whole thing put into a oven or something. But for $480 it don't make sense.

"That's a paperweight made of semi-precious stones fused together under tremendous pressure," she explains slowly, with her hands doing the mining and all the factory work.

"So what's a paperweight?" asks Rosie Giraffe.

"To weigh paper with, dumbbell," say Flyboy, the wise man from the East.

"Not exactly," say Miss Moore, which is what she say when you warm or way off too. "It's to weigh paper down so it won't scatter and make your desk untidy." So right away me and Sugar curtsy to each other and then to Mercedes who is more the tidy type.

"We don't keep paper on top of the desk in my class," say Junebug, figuring Miss Moore crazy or lyin one.

"At home, then," she say. "Don't you have a calendar and a pencil case and a blotter and a letter-opener on your desk at home where you do your homework?" And she know damn well what our homes look like cause she nosys around in them every chance she gets.

"I don't even have a desk," say Junebug. "Do we?"

"No. And I don't get no homework neither," says Big Butt.

"And I don't even have a home," say Flyboy like he do at school to keep the white folks off his back and sorry for him. Send this poor kid to camp posters, is his specialty.

"I do," says Mercedes. "I have a box of stationery on my desk and a picture of my cat. My godmother bought the stationery and the desk. There's a big rose on each sheet and the envelopes smell like roses."

"Who wants to know about your smelly-ass stationery," say Rosie Giraffe fore I can get my two cents in.

"It's important to have a work area all your own so that . . ."

"Will you look at this sailboat, please," say Flyboy, cuttin her off and pointin to the thing like it was his. So once again we tumble all over each other to gaze at this magnificent thing in the toy store which is just big enough to maybe sail two kittens across the pond if you strap them to the posts tight. We all start reciting the price tag like we in assembly. "Hand-crafted sailboat of fiberglass at one thousand one hundred ninety-five dollars."

"Unbelievable," I hear myself say and am really stunned. I read it again for myself just in case the group recitation put me in a trance. Same thing. For some reason this pisses me off. We look at Miss Moore and she lookin at us, waiting for I dunno what.

"Who'd pay all that when you can buy a sailboat set for a quarter at Pop's, a tube of glue for a dime, and a ball of string for eight cents? It must have a motor and a whole lot else besides," I say. "My sailboat cost me about fifty cents."

"But will it take water?" say Mercedes with her smart ass.

"Took mine to Alley Pond Park once," say Flyboy. "String broke. Lost it. Pity."

"Sailed mine in Central Park and it keeled over and sank. Had to ask my father for another dollar."

"And you got the strap," laugh Big Butt. "The jerk didn't even have a string on it. My old man wailed on his behind."

Little Q.T. was staring hard at the sailboat and you could see he wanted it bad. But he too little and somebody'd just take it from him. So what the hell. "This boat for kids, Miss Moore?"

"Parents silly to buy something like that just to get all broke up," say Rosie Giraffe.

"That much money it should last forever," I figure.

"My father'd buy it for me if I wanted it."

"Your father, my ass," say Rosie Giraffe getting a chance to finally push Mercedes.

"Must be rich people shop here," say Q.T.

"You are a very bright boy," say Flyboy. "What was your first clue?" And he rap him on the head with the back of his knuckles, since Q.T. the only one he could get away with. Though Q.T. liable to come up behind you years later and get his licks in when you half expect it.

"What I want to know is," I says to Miss Moore though I never talk to her, I wouldn't give the bitch that satisfaction, "is how much a real boat costs? I figure a thousand'd get you a yacht any day."

"Why don't you check that out," she says, "and report back to the group?" Which really pains my ass. If you gonna mess up a perfectly good swim day least you could do is have some answers. "Let's go in," she say like she got something up her sleeve. Only she don't lead the way. So me and Sugar turn the corner to where the entrance is, but when we get there I kinda hang back. Not that I'm scared, what's there to be afraid of, just a toy store. But

I feel funny, shame. But what I got to be shamed about? Got as much right to go in as anybody. But somehow I can't seem to get hold of the door, so I step away from Sugar to lead. But she hangs back too. And I look at her and she looks at me and this is ridiculous. I mean, damn, I have never ever been shy about doing nothing or going nowhere. But then Mercedes steps up and then Rosie Giraffe and Big Butt crowd in behind and shove, and next thing we all stuffed into the doorway with only Mercedes squeezing past us, smoothing out her jumper and walking right down the aisle. Then the rest of us tumble in like a glued-together jigsaw done all wrong. And people lookin at us. And it's like the time me and Sugar crashed into the Catholic church on a dare. But once we got in there and everything so hushed and holy and the candles and the bowin and the handkerchiefs on all the drooping heads, I just couldn't go through with the plan. Which was for me to run up to the altar and do a tap dance while Sugar played the nose flute and messed around in the holy water. And Sugar kept givin me the elbow. Then later teased me so bad I tied her up in the shower and turned it on and locked her in. And she'd be there till this day if Aunt Gretchen hadn't finally figured I was lyin about the boarder takin a shower.

Same thing in the store. We all walkin on tiptoe and hardly touchin the games and puzzles and things. And I watched Miss Moore who is steady watchin us like she waitin for a sign. Like Mama Drewery watches the sky and sniffs the air and takes note of just how much slant is in the bird formation. Then me and Sugar bump smack into each other, so busy gazing at the toys, 'specially the sailboat. But we don't laugh and go into our fat-lady bump-stomach routine. We just stare at that price tag. Then Sugar run a finger over the whole boat. And I'm jealous and want to hit her. Maybe not her, but I sure want to punch somebody in the mouth.

"Whatcha bring us here for, Miss Moore?"

"You sound angry, Sylvia. Are you mad about something?" Givin me one of them grins like she tellin a grown-up joke that never turns out to be funny. And she's lookin very closely at me like maybe she plannin to do my portrait from memory. I'm mad, but I won't give her that satisfaction. So I slouch around the store bein very bored and say, "Let's go."

Me and Sugar at the back of the train watchin the tracks whizzin by large then small then gettin gobbled up in the dark. I'm thinkin about this tricky toy I saw in the store. A clown that somersaults on a bar then does chin-ups just cause you yank lightly at his leg. Cost $35. I could see me askin my mother for a $35 birthday clown. "You wanna who that costs what?" she'd say, cocking her head to the side to get a better view of the hole in my head. Thirty-five dollars could buy new bunk beds for Junior and Gretchen's boy. Thirty-five dollars and the whole household could go visit Grand-daddy Nelson in the country. Thirty-five dollars would pay for the rent and the piano bill too. Who are these people that spend that much for performing clowns and $1000 for toy sailboats? What kinda work they do and how they live and how come we ain't in on it? Where we are is who we are, Miss Moore always pointin out. But it don't necessarily have to be that way, she always adds then waits for somebody to say that poor people have to wake up and demand their share of the pie and don't none of us know what kind of pie she talking about in the first damn place. But she ain't so smart cause I still got her four dollars from the taxi and she sure ain't gettin it messin up my day with this shit. Sugar nudges me in my pocket and winks.

Miss Moore lines us up in front of the mailbox where we started from, seem like years ago, and I got a headache for thinkin so hard. And we lean all over each other so we can hold up under the draggy ass lecture she always finishes us off with at the end before we thank her for borin us to tears. But she just looks at us like she readin tea leaves. Finally she say, "Well, what did you think of FAO Schwarz?"

Rosie Giraffe mumbles, "White folks crazy."

"I'd like to go there again when I get my birthday money," says Mercedes, and we shove her out the pack so she has to lean on the mailbox by herself.

"I'd like a shower. Tiring day," say Flyboy.

Then Sugar surprises me by sayin, "You know, Miss Moore, I don't think all of us here put together eat in a year what that sailboat costs." And Miss Moore lights up like somebody goosed her. "And?" she say, urging Sugar on. Only I'm standin on her foot so she don't continue.

"Imagine for a minute what kind of society it is in which some people can spend on a toy what it would cost to feed a family of six or seven. What do you think?"

"I think," say Sugar pushing me off her feet like she never done before cause I whip her ass in a minute, "that this is not much of a democracy if you ask me. Equal chance to pursue happiness means an equal crack at the dough, don't it?" Miss Moore is besides herself and I am disgusted with Sugar's treachery. So I stand on her foot one more time to see if she'll shove me. She shuts up, and Miss Moore looks at me, sorrowfully I'm thinkin. And somethin weird is goin on, I can feel it in my chest. "Anybody else learn anything today?" lookin dead at me. I walk away and Sugar has to run to catch up and don't even seem to notice when I shrug her arm off my shoulder.

"Well, we got four dollars anyway," she says. "Uh hun."

"We could go to Hascombs and get half a chocolate layer and then go to the Sunset and still have plenty money for potato chips and ice cream sodas."

"Uh hun."

"Race you to Hascombs," she say.

We start down the block and she gets ahead which is O.K. by me cause I'm going to the West End and then over to the Drive to think this day through. She can run if she want to and even run faster. But ain't nobody gonna beat me at nuthin.

DISCUSSION QUESTIONS

1. "'Where we are is who we are,' Miss Moore always pointin out." Is this "the lesson" that the title references? What do you take away from Miss Moore's field trip? What are the unique power dynamics between teacher and her students?

2. Throughout "The Lesson," there are scenes in which classism is brought to the forefront. How do the young people interpret the economic inequality in their life? How do they resist it?

3. Consider Sylvia's friend Sugar and other secondary characters. What role do they play in the story?

4. Can you recall a lesson in your youth that did or did not get through to you? Discuss.

Dance for Me

Amina Gautier

Originally published in 2006

Nadira was the other black girl in our class. She'd been at the school since kindergarten, while I'd come in seventh grade on a scholarship.

The girls on Lexington had it the worst. Hated maroon skirts the color of dried blood. Navy blazers complete with gaudy emblem. Goldenrod blouses with Peter Pan collars. And knee socks. Actually, knee socks weren't so bad. Knee socks served their purpose in the winter, keeping sturdy calves warm.

The girls on East End wore gray or navy skirts, plain and not pleated, with a white blouse, sweater optional.

Multiple skirts were another way to go. We had our choice of navy, gray, maroon and an unpleated light blue seersucker meant only for the spring. The choices allowed us to pretend we weren't really wearing a uniform. We merely hoped to be thought eccentric. Girls with fetishes for skirts with panels. But we fooled no one. Our clothing, our talk, our walk, our avid interest in grooming, and normal people's clothing, and daily preoccupation with what we would wear on upcoming field trips when allowed to be out of uniform, filled our time and talk. We had a special way of standing that was part lean, part slouch, as if posture were too much of a bother to consider.

Nameless, faceless on a school trip, we stood out. Solid-colored blouses, pleated skirts, knee socks, loafers, bluchers, or oxfords. Private school girls. Not to be confused with Catholic school girls. Or reform school girls (how many times did the kids in my neighborhood look at me in condescending pity?). Not to be confused with the girls from *The Facts of Life*. They were boarders. No matter how many times I tried to explain this, the kids in my neighborhood persisted in calling me Tootie.

We attended a second-tier all-girls' school. We weren't as illustrious as the private schools on the Upper East Side, yet not as seedy as the ones in Midtown. We clung to our small but unique differences. For example, having our choice of uniforms made us the envy of the other all-girls' schools. Girls were sure to take it out on us during soccer games. Secondly, there was our partnership with a nearby all-boys' school, our "brother" school two blocks away, which allowed us to have kissing partners whenever we put on a play.

At school, there were the WASPs and the JAPs. And me. Girls with last names for first names. Riley. Taylor. Haley. Morgan. Hayden. Girls whose names are meant for a boy or girl, depending.

I'd never told anyone this, but I always felt naked in my pleated skirt, vulnerable. There was a trick to rolling the skirt that would take several inches off, a way of rolling tightly and minutely that would allow one to hide the extra material beneath a fold of a shirt if one tucked one's shirt in properly, then pulled out just enough material to camouflage the extra skirt. Only I didn't know it. I'd seen it numerous times, jealously watching girls enter the bathroom with skirts that covered their knees and walk back out with skirts that skimmed their thighs, but I still couldn't get it. The lines of my pleats were never quite right, always drooping in the front, making me look slightly off kilter.

IT WAS LUNCHTIME and I was in the school's bathroom with my stomach bared to the mirror, trying to roll my skirt, when Taylor and Ashley entered and headed for the stalls, deep in conversation. Neither of them noticed me.

"Well, I wouldn't go with a guy from Buckley, that's for sure."

"I might not get to go at all. We're supposed to go to the Hamptons and my dad really has his heart set on it. How am I supposed to get out of it?"

"I don't know. I so need a new pair of jeans. Do you want to go to the Gap today after we get out of chorus?"

"Um, yeah. Hey, did you hear Heather's parents let Chase go to Cabo San Lucas with her for spring break?"

"No."

"They even paid his way."

So caught up in eavesdropping on their conversation, I didn't hear the squeal of the bathroom door the second time it opened. Heather walked in alone and went straight to the mirror. She frowned slightly when she heard herself being discussed. Then she went into a stall near theirs.

"Who said that?"

"Heather, that's who."

"I heard she broke up with him."

"For the coxswain? That's like way over."

"What happened?"

"He dumped her for a girl from Chapin."

Two toilets flushed simultaneously. By the time Taylor and Ashley emerged, I'd whipped out my Carmex and pretended to be carefully moisturizing, all thoughts of fixing my skirt gone. They washed their hands and walked out without looking at me. Once they left, Heather came out of her stall.

Moments like these were common. They happened several times during the day—self-reflective moments when girls met between classes, gathering in bathrooms and on stairways to consider the grave issues of the times and their place in the world. Usually the person being discussed wasn't present.

Heather was still standing there. Her eyes met mine in the mirror. "It's not true, you know."

"What?"

"I never went out with that guy. Never even kissed him. He was a total turd."

I shrugged. "Okay."

She scrutinized me. "You're in my class."

I nodded. "Yeah."

"Do you know about the party on West 91st this Friday?"

"At Trinity?"

"Are you going?"

I pretended to give the question some thought. The parties were hosted by coed private day schools that issued invitations to certain schools, which then issued memberships to certain students. She knew I couldn't go. The memberships were a subtle way of excluding the undesirables. The membership lists went out in sixth grade. The scholarship girls who came in through the enrichment programs started in seventh grade. There was no way ever to be included on the lists, unless someone sponsored me, which no one ever did. I had no plans to go to the party this Friday or any other Friday, and she knew it.

"I wasn't planning on it," I said.

"Oh. Do you know how to do that new dance they're doing?" she asked me. "You know the one that goes like this." Heather's gyrations resembled nothing I could identify.

"Um no, I can't say that I know that one," I said. "Sorry."

"Maybe I'm doing it wrong," she said.

"Maybe."

"It's called Running something."

"The Running Man?"

"That's it!" She touched my arm. "Do you know it?"

"Sure."

"Can you show me?"

I looked around. "Here? In the bathroom?"

"Yeah." Heather smiled at me, warm and eager. I really didn't want to. I wasn't a very good dancer and I didn't like to perform. At home, I would only sing in the shower, and I danced at house parties only when the lights were very low. But I danced for her, awkward at first since there was no music, but she didn't seem to notice or mind. Once I started dancing, her eyes never met mine. They were riveted instead to my legs and feet. I had a feeling she wanted to take notes.

"That looks so hard," she said.

"It's not," I huffed. I danced harder, wanting to show off. I was silently repeating the words of a popular song in my head to give myself a beat. I danced harder as I tried to incorporate moves I'd seen on *Video Music Box*, getting ahead of myself and quickly losing the beat. A video diva I had never been, watching videos only on Saturdays when my mother was out. I was losing my rhythm and running out of breath when she finally said, "Wow. You're good. Really, really good."

I stopped and took a deep breath. I smiled. "Thanks."

THAT EVENING, our phone rang, something it hardly ever did. My mother eyed the phone suspiciously, letting it ring three times before picking up. "Hello?" she answered warily, frowning at the unseen offender who'd interrupted her silence. "Yes, hold on." She held the phone out to me. "It's for you?" I ignored the question in her voice and grabbed it.

"Hi, it's me."

"Hi."

"It's Heather," she said, as if I wouldn't know her voice.

"Hey."

Who is it? my mother mouthed silently.

Heather, I mouthed back. *From school.*

It had been my mother's idea to put me in the enrichment program that had given me a scholarship for the all-girls' school, a decision she'd come to regret in the face of my loneliness and unpopularity. Now, she hovered and tried to listen in, filled with hope.

Heather's excitement came through, giddy and loud. "You're coming! You are so coming," she shrieked into my ear.

"What are you talking about?"

"The party this Friday. Did you forget?"

"No, I remember."

"Well, I got you in. I sponsored you," she said. There was a pause in her voice, as if she were waiting for something.

"Thanks," I said.

"You don't sound excited."

"I am."

"You are going to go, right?"

I didn't answer. I was taking my time to think about it. Although she'd sponsored me, there was still the question of clothing. I had nothing suitable to wear. The dance would also end late and I didn't think my mother would want me riding home from Manhattan to Brooklyn that late at night by myself. "Well—"

"Nadira is going," Heather said, as if it made a difference.

Nadira was the other black girl in our class. She'd been at the school since kindergarten, while I'd come in seventh grade on a scholarship. Although there were a number of affluent black and Asian girls in my school who'd been attending since kindergarten, I was not one of them and we claimed no kinship with one another. If I closed my eyes and listened to them speak, I wouldn't know they weren't white. Though Nadira and I belonged to the same race, she had more in common with the white girls. She and they lived in the same neighborhoods, had the same friends, values, and ideals. They listened to Z100 and sang classical in the choir. Like the white girls, she could not dance. I couldn't either, but no one knew that. They all took it for granted that I could.

"I'd like to, but I don't think my mom will let me because it ends so late."

"Tell her that's no problem. I wanted you to stay over. I'm having a little get-together at my house after the dance. You know, an after-the-party party. Just a couple of girls. A sleepover. Taylor. Maya. Ashley and maybe some others. Ask your mom if it's okay."

I held the receiver to my chest. "Mom? Heather wants to know if it's okay if I sleep over at her house this Friday." Heather lived in a penthouse on 95th and Park. Of course it was okay.

HEATHER INVITED ME to sit with her at lunch the next day. Four girls smiled at me as I sat, and they continued on with their discussions.

"I have this body suit and I'm going to wear it with my white jeans," Maya said. The other girls nodded their approval.

"You should wear your hair half up and half down," Heather told her.

"I don't have anything to wear. I'm going to need something new," Taylor said.

"Let's go to the Gap after class today and find something," Ashley suggested.

They were all wearing fleeced pullovers in different colors from L.L. Bean or Patagonia over their collared blouses and heather gray leggings beneath their pleated skirts. None of them had on socks. Their feet were bare in their loafers, docksiders, and bluchers.

I excused myself to go to the bathroom. There, I peeled off my socks. Ashley followed behind me. When I stood up, socks, in hand, she said, "Um, do you think you could show me the dance you showed Heather?"

THE NEXT DAY, I was back in the bathroom, showing five new girls. For the next two days, Heather brought girls to me and we took them into the bathroom to teach them the steps. For the next two days, I danced and danced on the cold white tiles while white girls leaned against sinks and stall doors and watched. The dancing, I thought, brought me respect and admiration. Through it, I was redeeming myself in their eyes. I was, after all these years, good for something.

THE DAY BEFORE the dance, Heather caught me on my way out to the train station. "I've been meaning to tell you this. About the party on Friday." Hands jammed into her jacket pockets, she stood on one foot, the other snaked around her calf, rubbing the back of her leg with the toe of her shoe.

My stomach tightened. Now she'd tell me it had all been a joke. They'd been teasing me. Making me feel as though I fit in was a prank some upperclasswoman had put them up to. "What about it?"

"Well, I know I told you there were just going to be girls at the party, but I wanted to make sure you'd come. There are going to be a few guys there, too. Don't worry, they're cool. They're guys I know from St. Bernard's, Allen-Stevenson, Buckley, and Collegiate."

"But—"

"They're going to sleep in the den. We'll meet them at the party and they'll come back with us. Is that cool?"

"Yeah," I said, relieved that her groundbreaking news had nothing to do with me.

"Good. Look, the girls and I chipped in on this. We were wondering if you could score us some weed? We want to have some real fun. I hope this is enough," Heather said, pressing crinkly bills into my hand. She patted my arm and stepped off the curb to hail a cab to take her home. I clutched the money in my hand, walked down Lexington to catch the 4 train, and rode home.

WHEN I GOT HOME that night, I searched in my mother's sewing basket until I found her seam ripper. I removed the deadly thing and carefully pulled off the stitches surrounding the little horse on the back pocket of my jeans.

I changed into these jeans, a trial run for the real test tomorrow. I was surprised to see myself in regular clothes. I changed shirts and threw on a light jacket. I counted out the money Heather had given me, then folded it neatly and slipped it into my pocket.

"Where are you going?" my mother asked when she saw me at the door.

"Out."

She didn't ask for any further explanation. Something had changed between us ever since the phone call. My blossoming friendships pleased her. My mother was as happy as if the invitation had been extended to her. Just yesterday, she'd put her hand on my shoulder while I was washing dishes. "I just want you to be happy," she'd said, her guilt now assuaged.

There was a store two blocks away that I knew was just a front. I'd gone in once to buy snacks and everything they sold me was expired, stale. I pushed through the door and walked in. One teenager hunched over an arcade game and two lounged against the corners of the wall. Twenty-five-cent bags of popcorn, potato chips, and cheese curls, ten-cent lollipops and five-cent Peanut Chews and Super Bubbles were behind a counter covered in Plexiglas.

I walked up to the counter.

"Can I buy some weed here?"

I could feel everyone look at me. The man behind the counter squinted. He cleared his throat. He took a long time before he spoke. "We got soda and chips. What you see, that's what we got."

"But I want to buy some weed," I said. "I have money."

"We sell candy, soda, and chips," he said. "You wanna buy some candy?"

I didn't know what else to do. I was frustrated, wanting to argue. He knew it was a weed spot; I knew it was a weed spot. Was there some magic word I needed to say, some secret code that would let him know I meant business?

I pulled my money out and held it up to the Plexiglas. "Open sesame," I said.

He shook his head. I walked out.

A minute later, I felt someone behind me. I turned. I recognized him from the store; he'd been playing Pac-Man. "What was you doing in there? You crazy or something?"

I walked faster. "Leave me alone."

"That was real stupid. What, you not from around here?"

"I live here," I told him.

He didn't believe me. "Where?"

"Miller and Pitkin."

"I live on that block and I never seen you."

"Well, I go to school," I said.

His lips curled up then. They were full, made brown from smoking. His eyes were large, round, sleepy. He was older. Beautiful. I felt my mistake. "I didn't mean it like that."

He walked by my side. "So why you wanna buy weed?"

"Just to try it," I said. "For fun."

"You ever smoke a blunt before?"

"I didn't want a blunt. I wanted a joint."

He looked at me like I was stupid. "I was going to buy it for my friends," I said. "They asked me to get it for a party."

"So, you still want it?"

"Five dollars for a nickel bag, right?"

"You been watching too much TV," he said.

HE REFUSED to give it to me out on the street.

"Let's take a walk." We walked past my block and past the intermediate school to the park.

He stopped when we got to the swings. He sat down on one and backpedaled with his feet. "Come here."

I stood between his legs; we were eye to eye.

"What's your name?" he asked.

"You don't need to know."

He nodded. "So, you like white boys."

"No," I said.

"Black guys?"

"Nope."

"Girls?" he asked, his voice filled with disbelief and excitement.

"I don't like anybody," I said.

He pulled me towards him and kissed me. The faint sweet scent of smoke clung to his chin and I knew that I would smell of him. I had a feeling as if I were waiting in the subway for my train just before it pulls in and it was rushing down the track, blowing its dirty hot wind underneath my skirt, caressing the bare skin between pleats and socks. I tried to pull away but felt his hands on me cupping my butt, felt him slip the bag of weed into my back pocket. He turned me away from him, adjusting me so that I sat on his front thighs. Pretending to put his arms around me, he slipped his hands into my front pockets, seeking until he found my folded cash. Slick, I thought. Smooth. To anyone passing by, we looked like two fools making out in the park.

THE PARTY, because I had longed for it, was a disappointment. The DJ could not mix one song into another. The lights never got very low. We stood in a papered gymnasium, in jeans, stretchy shirts, and too many coats of mascara. Girls from different schools divided themselves accordingly. Even without their uniforms, I could pick out the girls from Brearley, Chapin, and Spence. The boys Heather knew didn't show up until the end of the party. The only people I really knew were Heather, Taylor, Maya, and Ashley, and every time I saw them, they were all dancing, proudly showing off the moves I'd taught them. I ran into Nadira once that night when we were both getting sodas, but she didn't speak to me. I held up the wall all night. No one asked me to dance. I held my plastic cup of soda and thought of my mother at home, sleeping blissfully, happy and proud.

I only had one chance to talk to Heather at the dance. She came over to where I stood on the wall, her face flushed from dancing. "Did I do okay?" she asked me.

"You look good," I said.

"How do you like it?"

I shrugged. "It's okay."

"Aren't you dancing?"

"Nobody asked me."

"They probably don't want you to embarrass them," Heather said. I didn't bother to tell her that the dance I'd shown her was the only one I knew. "Don't worry," she said. "The real party starts when we get to my house."

AT HEATHER'S HOUSE, we had carte blanche. Her parents were asleep. Heather brought out the alcohol, I pulled out the small bag of weed, and we wasted no time getting drunk and high. A boy Heather had introduced as Gabe wanted to play a version of Spin the Bottle.

I was the first victim. Gabe and I looked at each other across the thin neck of the bottle, unsure.

"He's never made it with a black girl before," Taylor said.

"So?"

"Go in the closet with him," Heather suggested. "Show him how it's done." She clapped me on the arm and gave me a push. Gabe held out his hand and I got up, unsteadily taking it. I wasn't sure that I wanted to go, but I went.

We sat in the deep closet; the hems of Heather's jackets grazed the tops of our heads. I decided I couldn't, wouldn't do it. Gabe slid a finger up my arm and I shivered, backing away. "Wow, this closet is really big, huh?"

"It's cool," he said. "We don't have to, you know, I mean unless you want . . ." He looked hopeful even in the dark.

"I can't," I said.

"Maybe if you touch it." He took my hand and rubbed it against his denim crotch, his hand over mine.

"I'm going to be sick," I said.

"Whoa, wait a minute," he said. "Okay."

"Sick sick sick," I said.

He leaned back, but in a minute he asked, "Can I touch your breasts?"

"I don't think so."

"Just once?" He reached under my shirt. My bra was lace, one of my mother's castoffs. My underwear did not match, but I knew he would never know that.

"Hey," he said, feeling the lace cups of my bra. "Whoa. Hey."

"Whoa. Hey," I said, mocking him, feeling suddenly warm.

His hand closed over my breast and squeezed. It made me think of the old-fashioned cars in a Bugs Bunny cartoon. "Beep beep," I said, then burst out laughing. He laughed too and then the two of us couldn't stop laughing. We fell against each other, laughing. Then he pulled me through the jackets and across his lap, pushing his tongue into my mouth, banging his teeth against mine, kissing me wet and sloppy. I tasted the strong flavor of weed on his tongue and thought of the boy who'd sold it to me, how beautiful he'd been, how though we lived just a few blocks apart, we were strangers. Like the boy pressing himself against me, we were from two different worlds. They were both from the real world, their own distinct ones, but I was somewhere in limbo. Set apart, I didn't know how to let either of them in.

I knew Gabe's hands were tugging my shirt down, that in a minute they'd be working the latch of my bra, but I didn't stop him. In the dark of Heather's closet, I tried to see what Gabe saw. I pictured an image of myself that was Heather's body and face, only it was black and it was me. I saw how much of me would change; I saw the girl I would become. And I decided to go ahead and miss myself right now, knowing that the girl I would become wouldn't know how to appreciate me at all.

DISCUSSION QUESTIONS

1. "Moments like these were common. They happened several times during the day—self-reflective moments when girls met between classes, gathering in bathrooms and on stairways to consider the grave issues of the times and their place in the world. Usually the person being discussed wasn't present." Consider the role of gossip in this story. How does it contribute—or detract—from the narrator's sense of belonging?

2. How does Gautier explore peer pressure? What did you take away from the narrator's experience? Consider the difference between performing one's identity and experiencing genuine self-transformation with respect to the different characters in the short story.

Bad Behavior

Alexia Arthurs

Originally published in 2016

Before she had children, she had hoped that she would
see her daughter as more than a daughter, as a person
with desires and her own set of truths, but it turned
out that all she saw was a child who needed from her.

P am and Curtis brought Stacy to Jamaica because they
didn't know what else to do with her. They believed that
her old-time granny would straighten her out. In Brooklyn, Stacy cut her classes often, and she was caught giving a boy
a blowjob in an empty classroom. They looked at the sweet little face on the body of a woman, and they were terrified of her
and for her. It seemed that her breasts and ass were getting bigger every day. Often Pam would pull down Stacy's shirt to give
her ass better coverage, and Stacy would groan and laugh, tuck-
ing her shirt back into her jeans. Pam wondered aloud to Curtis whether Stacy's curvy body was because of all the chicken
wings she enjoyed eating from the Chinese restaurant. In America, Pam argued, chickens were injected with hormones, which

could explain all the little black girls with breasts and asses before their time. Stacy refused to eat breakfast because she was never hungry in the mornings, and because the school lunch was "nasty," she was ravenous by the end of the school day. She would come home with a takeout box: pork fried rice and fried chicken wings. She ate while she did her homework—somehow, in the midst of teenage angst and man hunger, she remained a diligent student—and later she would refuse to eat dinner with her parents and little brother because she was still full. Recently, Curtis was driving on Rockaway Parkway when he saw Stacy walk out of the train station, just come from school. A man, not a boy, but a man in baggy jeans, just any old street thug, had called to his daughter, and she had actually turned around and walked back to him. They were still talking when Curtis showed up to escort Stacy home. Pam and Curtis were afraid of their fourteen-year-old daughter. Often they would tell each other that this was what America did to children. This blasted country that turned parents into children and children into parents! One need not look any further than the white people on television who asked their children what they wanted to eat for dinner. In Jamaica, children knew to respect adults, while it wasn't unusual to hear an American child call an adult by her first name. It wasn't that Jamaican children were perfect—it was that when they made mistakes, they knew to be ashamed. All children were selfish, but American ones had an easier time living for themselves.

They took their daughter to Jamaica on the pretense of a vacation. Before they left Brooklyn, when Pam checked Stacy's suitcase, she found that her daughter had packed two name-plate necklaces that read BAD BITCH and FLAWLESS, and some thongs that Pam didn't know she owned. Pam left the "flawless"

necklace in the suitcase and hid the "bad bitch" necklace and
thongs. Stacy didn't seem to notice the missing items. On the
beach, she wore sunglasses and the two-piece bathing suit she'd
bought with her own money, revealing the belly button piercing her parents didn't know she had. When a dreadlocked man
saw her sitting on the beach by herself, he invited her to follow
him to his house. She had looked into the man's face and kissed
her teeth without fear as though he and she were size. Every
day, Stacy climbed the mango tree behind her grandma's house
and then she ate several mangoes in one sitting. In the afternoons, she walked down to the shop to buy banana chips, even
though she had five unopened packages sitting on the dresser,
because she liked that the boy at the counter flirted with her
and looked openly at her breasts.

On the fifth day, while Stacy slept, her parents and little
brother left. A few hours later, her grandmother, Trudy, nudged
her out of bed, asking, "Yuh goin' sleep di whole day?" She
was eating the saltfish and dumplings her grandmother made
for breakfast when she thought to ask about her parents and
brother. It wasn't the first morning she'd awakened late to hear
that they'd started the day without her. At first, Trudy ignored
her, so Stacy asked again. "Yuh nah be'ave yuhself," her grandmother told her, speaking quietly and carefully, "so dey lef' yuh
wid me until yuh can be'ave yuhself." Stacy behaved very badly,
cussing up some bad words and throwing her breakfast on the
floor, which surprised the old lady so much that all she could say
was "Jesus Christ." She hadn't believed the girl was as bad as
they said, and since she was lonely living in that house by herself,
she'd gladly welcomed her. Stacy ran to the front of the house
and looked down the road to see if they had only recently left.

She knew this couldn't be the case, but she looked anyway. Then she went to the back of the house, behind the old pit toilet, so that she could cry without anyone seeing her. She bawled for a long time. She punched her fist into the walls of the long-retired pit toilet, but the pain only made her cry harder. She felt someone watching, and when she looked down, Fatty, her grandmother's mongrel dog, was looking up at her. She bent to rub Fatty's belly, which was heavy with puppies, and the dog reached up to lick the tears from her face.

Over the first two weeks after her parents left, Stacy's spirit softened. She was quieter, more inward. When she spoke to her parents on the phone, she promised that she would behave herself. But Curtis and Pam weren't ready to let Stacy back into their home. There were times they missed her—she was, after all, a sweet girl when she wanted to be, and she was the first-born, which meant they loved her in a different—not necessarily better—way than they loved their son, Curtis Jr., a chubby ten-year-old who was an easy child. They told her that after a year, if she improved, she could come home.

EVENTUALLY, TRUDY BROUGHT UP Stacy's bad behavior back in New York: "Yuh such ah pretty girl fi do some ugly tings. Why yuh won' be'ave yuhself?" And Stacy had smiled and looked embarrassed because she was shy for her grandmother to know certain things about her, and yet it was a compliment to hear that she was pretty. She'd been afraid when she put her mouth on the boy's penis. Patrick was one of the most desired boys in school, and of all the other girls, he had pulled Stacy into an empty classroom, putting her hand down his pants so that she could touch his penis. This happened a few times, them kissing in empty classrooms, and one day he pushed his fingers down her jeans, and eventually she climaxed, and it was surprising and gratifying because she had never masturbated before and hadn't known that a boy's fingers could do that to her. She told one of her friends and the friend had been surprised to hear that Stacy hadn't reciprocated, and this made Stacy feel as though she'd done something wrong. She was sure that Patrick would never pull her into a classroom again, and when he did, she wanted to make it so that he wouldn't be disappointed. The first and only time, she was caught. Her parents had been furious, and they had said all kinds of things, but they hadn't asked why.

Every morning, Trudy woke her granddaughter so that she could help with the breakfast, and she would help with the other meals as well. Stacy learned to fry dumplings that were almost as good as her grandmother's, to make a nice chicken foot soup, and to bake sweet potato pudding. In New York, Pam had done all the cooking. When Stacy started at the all-girls high school, she learned to wash her uniform by hand even though Trudy had a washing machine, because her grandmother claimed that it was the only way to ensure that a white shirt was really clean. She was distracted from boys because the relationships with her classmates were so intricate and consuming, all of them interested in befriending the foreign girl.

The mother Trudy had been was another woman. When Pam was sixteen, Trudy, acting on a tip from a neighbor, had found a love letter in one of her daughter's schoolbooks and had punched her, even slapped her face. It wasn't until Pam had become a woman with a husband and children that she could almost forgive her mother. Not all mothers could afford to be kind. When

Pam had first come to America, she cleaned for a white family, and one afternoon, standing at her employer's bedroom door, she overheard the woman and her teenage daughter debate the daughter's decision to lose her virginity to her boyfriend. Pam marveled that this was a thing that could happen. She had vowed to become a better mother than Trudy. But then, without realizing until it was too late, without knowing why or how, she had failed her daughter. She had had to send her daughter to her mother, and she hoped that the old woman would be tough. Maybe, she thought, maybe the formula so many Caribbean mothers use on their daughters wasn't the worst thing. Maybe, she thought, it was sacrilege for daughters to discuss their sex lives with their mothers, and what a daughter needed was not a confidante but a woman who loved her enough to show her some of the harshness that the world was ready and able to give her.

For a long time after Pam came to America, it seemed that she was eternally in school. At first, for years, she studied on a part-time basis for her bachelor's degree. After all, she hadn't come to America to clean and cook for white people and take care of their children. After marrying Curtis, she went to school to become a registered nurse. It had taken longer than necessary because she had to attend part-time. She needed an income, so she was still cleaning for white people and taking care of their children. When Stacy was growing up, Pam was always working overtime so that they could buy a house. And when she and Curtis bought a house, she worked overtime so that they could pay the mortgage, the water bill, the electric bill, and all the other bills that came with owning a house. She'd married a man who wasn't as ambitious as she was. For years, she nagged Curtis to go to school, and for years he said that he would look about it soon but soon never came. He was a simple man when she'd met him, and she believed that he would be good to her, so she married him for something that wasn't quite love and because she was tired of struggling in America without a green card. When she met him, he made his money by cleaning for the church he attended, and though it wasn't plenty of money, he seemed contented. Now he was one of the janitors at an elementary school. If it had been up to Curtis, she and the children would have stayed in that tiny two-bedroom on Sterling Street and he wouldn't have minded. Curtis, unlike Pam, hadn't come to America for a better life. He'd left Jamaica because his mother had filed for him, and he figured that it seemed like a reasonable opportunity. Pam worked hard because she had to—what choice did she have with a husband like Curtis? If she didn't put a pot on the stove, the thought would never have occurred to him. Before she had children, she had hoped that she would see her daughter as more than a daughter, as a person with desires and her own set of truths, but it turned out that all she saw was a child who needed from her. She determined that what a daughter needed was to be fed, clothed, baptized, and protected from men. When her daughter put her mouth on that boy's penis, the question hadn't been why, but the answer had been no.

THE FOLLOWING YEAR, Pam, Curtis, and Curtis Jr. return to Jamaica. Pam leaves Curtis and Curtis Jr. to bring the suitcases into the house, while she goes looking for her daughter. The house is empty, so she ventures to the back, where Stacy is squatting under the mango tree, scaling a pan of fish. Pam watches her. Every time Stacy guts a fish, she throws the insides to Fatty.

In New York, her daughter had certainly never cleaned fish. Of course, Pam thinks, of course my mother set her right. Unbeknownst to her, Trudy talks to her granddaughter, reasons with her. Once, they'd walked down to the shop together and because Trudy noticed that the shopkeeper's son was looking at her granddaughter as though he had plans for her, she said to him, "Tek yuh eye off mi gran'pickney. Ah no yuh get Grace pickney pregnant?" Stacy had laughed in agreement. Now she looks up, and in her excitement to greet her mother, she knocks over the pan of fish, but Fatty, who is pregnant again, is quicker than she is, grabbing a fish in her mouth and ambling off before anyone can stop her.

DISCUSSION QUESTIONS

1. "All children were selfish, but American ones had an easier time living for themselves." What do you make of Stacy's parents sending her to Jamaica? Do you agree that Stacy's setting contributed to her "bad behavior"?

2. This story shares similar themes to Jamaica Kincaid's "Girl"—how to prepare food, manage chores, and stay in line. Compare and contrast the structures and messages of these stories.

3. When does Stacy feel most comfortable in her identity? At what point does she seem to feel the shame in the short story? What is the most surprising aspect of her transformation in Jamaica?

Love

Melvin in the Sixth Grade

Dana Johnson

Originally published in 2000

Two months since being the new girl myself, Melvin was the only one who called me by my name; otherwise the other kids usually named me after my hairstyle.

Maybe it was around the time that the Crips sliced up my brother's arm for refusing to join their gang. Or it could have been around the time that the Crips *and* the Bloods shot up the neighborhood one Halloween so we couldn't go trick-or-treating. It could have even been the time that my brother's friend, Anthony, got shot for being at the wrong place at the wrong time. But my father decided it was time to take advantage of a veteran's loan, get out of L.A., and move to the suburbs. Even if I can't quite nail the events that spurred the move, I know that one and a half months after I climbed into my father's rusted-out Buick Wildcat and said good-bye to 80th Street and hello to Vermillion Street with its lawns and streets without sidewalks, I fell for my first man.

From the day Mrs. Campbell introduced him to the class, reprimanded us for laughing at his name, and sat him down next to me, I was struck by Melvin Bukeford with his stiff jeans, white creases ironed down the middle, huge bell-bottoms that rang, the kids claimed, every time the bells knocked against each other. Shiny jeans because he *starched* them. Melvin sporting a crew cut in 1981 when everybody else had long scraggly hair like the guys in Judas Priest or Journey. Pointed ears that stuck out like Halloween fake ones. The way he dragged out every single last word on account of being from Oklahoma. The long pointed nose and the freckles splattered all over his permanently pink face. Taller than everybody else because he was thirteen.

All that and a new kid is why nobody liked him. Plus he had to be named Melvin. All us kids, we'd never seen anything like him before, not in school, not for real, not in California. And for me he was even more of a wonder because I was just getting used to the white folks in West Covina, the way they spoke, the clothes they wore. Melvin was even weirder to me than the rest of them. It was almost like he wasn't white. He was an alien of some kind. My beautiful alien from Planet Cowboy.

I was writing *Melvin Melvin Melvin Melvin, Mrs. Avery Arlington Bukeford* on my Pee Chee folder by Melvin's second week of school. We walked the same way home every single school day. I fell in love with the drawl of his voice, the way he forgot the "e" in Avery; "Av'ry," he said it soft, or "AV'ry" when he thought I'd said the funniest thing, squinting at me sideways and giving me that dimple in his left cheek. All that made me feel like, well, just like I wanted to kiss my pillow at night and call it Melvin. So I did. "Ohhh, Mellllvin," I said, making out with my pillow every night. "Ohhh yeahh, Melvin."

I was keeping all that a secret until my eighteen-year-old brother saw my folder one day and asked me who Melvin was. "None ya," I said, and he said he knew it had to be some crazy-looking white boy—or a Mexican, because that's all West Covina had.

"Avery's done gone white boy crazy!" he called out. "I'ma tell Daddy!"

I ran into my room and slammed the door to stare at my four bare walls because Daddy had made me take down the posters I'd had up, all centerfolds from *Teen Beat* and *Tiger Beat* magazines. For one glamorous week I had Andy Gibb, Shaun Cassidy, and Leif Garrett looking down on me while I slept. But one day Daddy passed my door, took one look at Leif Garrett all blonde and golden tan in his tight white jeans that showed off a *very* big bulge, and asked me, "Avery, who in the *hell* are all these white boys?"

"Oh, Daddy, that's just Andy—"

"Get that shit down off those walls right now," Daddy said. He glared at Leif Garrett.

I couldn't figure out why he was yelling at me. "But why—"

"What did I say?" he demanded.

"Take the posters down," I mumbled. And that's why I was staring at four blank walls.

But that was OK, because Melvin was my world. I didn't need him up on the wall. I had him in my head. I turned on the radio to listen to Ozzy Osbourne, who'd just bitten the head off a dove a few days before, singing about going off the rails on a crazy train.

———

TWO MONTHS SINCE being the new girl myself, Melvin was the only one who called me by my name; otherwise the other kids usually named me after my hairstyle. Like Minnie Mouse or Cocoa Puffs if I wore my hair in Afro puffs. Or Afro Sheen if my mother had greased my hair and pressed it into submission the night before. Or Electric Socket if I was wearing a plain old Afro. Avery. To hear that coming out of someone else's mouth at school was like hearing "Hey, Superstar."

They were warming up to me, though. Lisa White, who always smelled like pee, had invited me to her Disneyland party. Why, I don't know, but I was going, grateful to be going, For no reason, one day, she said, "Hey, you," when she saw me standing by the monkey bars watching her and a bunch of friends jumping rope. "Come to my party if you want to." What I heard was something like, "Hey you, you just won a trillion, bizillion, cabillion dollars."

But everything had become even more tricky than usual. Lisa didn't like Melvin. Nobody did.

One day when the smog wasn't so bad in the San Gabriel Valley (the air was only orange, not brown, and you could sort of see the mountains if you squeezed your eyes some), Melvin and I stopped at the same place we did every day after school: by the ivy in front of Loretta Morales's house on the corner, fat Loretta with feathered hair and green eyes, in high school now, even though we used to play Barbies together, who got down with boys now, who had a mother in a wheelchair for no reason I could figure out. She could walk, Mrs. Morales.

Melvin stuck his hand in the ivy, pulling at this and that, not finding what he was looking for. "Hmm," he said. "Av'ry girl, I b'lieve you done took my cigarettes for yourself, ain't you?"

"Nuh uh!" I grinned at him and hugged my folders and books to my chest. "You just ain't looking good."

"Well, then, help me out some." He brushed his hands through the ivy like he was running them through bathwater to test it.

"There's rats in there." I wasn't going to put my hands in the ivy because it was dark and I couldn't see. If I couldn't see, there was no need to just stick my hands into all that dark space like a crazy person, I didn't think.

Melvin took off his jean jacket and handed it to me. It had MEL spelled out on the back with silver studs you pressed into the fabric. He was getting serious about looking for those Winstons. I put my face in his jacket and smelled it, since he wasn't watching me. It smelled like smoke and sweat and general boy. From then on forever, I decided, I would love the smell of boy.

"Here we go," he said in a minute. He stood up, tapped the package on his palm, pulled out the cigarette, popped it in his mouth, took the match that always seemed to be tucked behind his ear, struck it on his boot, and cupped the match while he lit his smoke, so the fire wouldn't go out. He drew a deep suck on his cigarette and then threw his head back and blew the smoke up toward the sky. Then he rolled the packet of cigarettes in the sleeve of his white T-shirt. I watched all this like a miracle.

"I been dying for that cigarette all day long. You don't know," he said, letting it dangle between his lips. He winked at me. "Whoo weee!" he hollered.

But I did know. How it felt to want something so bad. Whoo weee, Melvin. How could *you* not know?

Melvin tried to take his jacket back. "I got it," I said.

He shrugged. "If you wont to."

But five steps later we were at my street. Verdugo. So I had to give the jacket back anyway.

"Hey, Melvin," I started, trying to kill time and keep him with me a little longer, "you going to Lisa White's Disneyland party?" But the second the words were out of my mouth, I knew it was the dumbest question I could have asked. Like Lisa would have asked Melvin to her party, like Lisa even *thought* about Melvin. That was just stupid to even think. How dumb *are* you? I asked myself.

Melvin took his cigarette out of his mouth and offered me a puff, he knew I wouldn't. We had that little joke going on between us. He got a kick out of me being a Goody Two-shoes and not taking a puff, even though I nearly died at the thought of my lips touching something that Melvin's lips touched. He grinned. "There's your brother," he said, trying to scare me about the cigarette, but I knew Owen was already at work.

"You ain't funny, Melvin Bukeford," I said, and punched him in the shoulder.

He rubbed it like it hurt. I guess I punched him harder than I thought. "Dang, Killer, you tough when you wont to be, ain't you?" He took another puff before he said, "Lisa ast me to go to her party, but I said I didn't b'lieve I could cause of the money, but shoot, I can steal me enough money to go to Disneyland, I just ain't too impressed with her or no Disneyland neither."

I could not believe what I was hearing. Lisa asked Melvin *and* he said no? I thought I was asked because I was liked—or on my way to be liked.

Melvin said, "She just askin everybody to say that everybody came to her little party. So what about her little pissy party." He stubbed out his cigarette. "Later, Miss Av'ry," he said, pulling on his jacket. "And don't be reaching into my stash of cigs else a big rat'll chew off your fingers."

"Nuh uh, Melvin!" I sang. I still stung from Lisa not really warming up to me that much after all, but Melvin's teasing and winking and dimples and smoke drifting hazy over his watery blue eyes made me happier. I would never need anything else in a man as long as I walked the planet earth. I watched him walk downhill in that odd slopey way he did, knees bending a little too deep at every step, like a flamingo. A flamingo smoking a cigarette wearing a studded denim jacket.

BY THE TIME I was walking through the door, home from school, Mama was running out the door to catch the bus to her first job at the sprinkler factory and later, her room-cleaning job, like always. I was only eleven but already taller than she was—and bigger all the way around. She was a little woman with a tiny neat Afro, but you didn't mess around and confuse the little and the tiny with the way she ran things. And with Daddy, when you saw big and tall, you didn't mess around with that either.

She didn't wait for me to speak before she started telling me what all I had to do. "... And the dishes, and put that pot of beans on. I already seasoned them. Don't put no more salt in them beans and mess em up, do and you know what you gone be in for. And your Aunt Rochelle sent you some more clothes. They in the living room. Be sweet." She patted me on the shoulders, hard, heavy so you could hear it even. Then she was out the door.

I was afraid to even look in the living room to see what kind of clothes were waiting for me. Aunt Rochelle's hand-me-downs from somebody's friend's cousin's daughter, used to be cool, but now that I was living in this new house in this new city far enough from L.A. that we were grateful when we saw other black people around town, I didn't like the hand-me-downs so much anymore because they were one more thing the kids could pick on me about. The fancy pants were Dittos or Chemin de Fers or Sergio Valentes or jackets that were Members Only. When they weren't calling me Afro Sheen they were calling me Polyester or Kmart, where I got my good clothes. Or they called me Welfare for getting in the "county" line when I lined up for my lunch from the free lunch program for people who needed it.

When I told my mother and father that I wanted different clothes, my mother said, "Chemin de Who for how much? You must be out your mind."

And of course I was. All eleven-year-olds were. I was out of my mind, especially for Melvin. Couldn't anybody understand that if I had just one cool outfit, like Melvin, I'd be on my way to the kids liking me for reals? Cool outfits may not have worked for Melvin, but he was an alien. I wasn't. If I tried hard enough, I'd be *in*. I found these lime-green polyester slacks that I really liked and put the rest of the clothes in the bottom of my bedroom closet. I imagined him saying, "Whoo wee, Av'ry! Check you out!"

MELVIN WAS GOING to get his ass kicked after school. I heard it from Terri Stovendorf, the tomboy with the protruding forehead and sharp teeth on the side like a dog. She got drunk behind the portables, cheap mobile add-ons to the rest of the elementary school. She was always pushing me around, making fun of the way I spoke. I didn't know there was anything wrong with the way I spoke. I said "prolly" when it was "probably." I said "fort" when they said "fart." I said I was "finna" go home and not "getting ready" to go home. That's how we'd always spoken and it was good enough until the suburbs. I started studying the kids and editing myself. *Mama*, I practiced in the mirror at home. *I'm go-eng to do my homework. Go-eng. Who farted? Somebody farted?*

"Groovy Jan and Cindy and Bobby and Marcia," Owen said, whenever he heard me. "Grue-vee."

When Terri told me the news, I was at the water fountain at recess taking a break from tetherball, trying to get some water from the warm trickle coming out. I had to put my lips right up against the spout and tried not to look at the gum somebody had stuck down by the drain. When I picked my head up and wiped the water from my mouth, Terri called me. "Hey, Burnt Toast."

I turned around.

"Nice pants."

"Really? Thanks." I smiled at her shyly.

"I was kidding, dumb-ass."

I scratched my scalp because I didn't know what else to do. I had eight neat cornrows that ran from my hairline to the base of my neck.

"Listen," Terri said, suddenly doing business. "You and that country cowboy guy are always going around." We said "going around" to mean dating. I smiled at the thought that people thought Melvin and I were together, even though I was still trying to keep my distance from him in front of other people. I was scared of having more wrath heaped on me.

"What are you smiling at, stupid?"

"We're not going together," I mumbled. I started kicking around a rock with my imitation Vans, which were cooler than cool sneakers. Mine were knockoffs from Kmart.

"No duh," Terri said. "Like Country Cowboy would even go around with a nigger. I meant, like, walking around and stuff."

I had been called so many names that even "nigger" didn't faze me anymore. Not so much anymore. There were Mexicans and Philippinos and Chinese kids sprinkled throughout the class, but they blended better than me. There was more than one of each of them, and when they were called "taco" when they were from Portugal or "chink," even when they happened to be Philippino or Korean, that was the best kids like Terri could do with them. With me, there seemed to be endless creativity. So all I said to Terri was "Melvin and me don't go around, walk around together. His house is on *my* way home."

"Whatever. He's going to get his ass kicked after school today, and you better not tell him."

"Why?"

"Because I'll kick your ass, too."

"No, I mean . . ." I started cracking my knuckles. A bad habit I still have. I finally left the rock alone. "I mean, why are y'all going to beat up Melvin?"

Terri looked at me with disgust and wonder, like I was eating my own boogers, like Casey McLaughlin did. He modeled kid underwear because he was good looking; long eyelashes like a deer, and lips that always looked like there was lipstick on them. You could see him in those color junk ads that were always shoved in every mailbox in the neighborhoods, and he was as stupid as a stick.

"Are you a total moron?" Terri ran her hands through her stringy brown hair and left before I could answer.

I went looking for Melvin to tell, but I couldn't be *seen* telling him. I saw him sitting on a swing, all alone. Spinning in one direction real fast to tighten the swing chains and then spinning the other way as fast as he could to get that dizzy rush. The playground was full: a bunch of kids were playing touch football in the field, all the tetherballs were taken, two dodgeball games were going on, and both of the handball courts were taken. I couldn't see Terri, or cross-eyed Eddie Chambers, or nasty Hector Hernandez, who was always grabbing himself and lapping his tongue in and out like a snake at the girls. They would all be the ringleaders after school. The coast seemed clear enough to warn Melvin, but before I could make my way over to him, somebody called me.

"Hey, Turd Head," Harry Collins called out to me, my name whenever I wore cornrows. "We need one more person for butt ball." He walked over toward me with the red rubber ball while I tried to figure out how to say no. Butt ball hurt. You and one other person had to volunteer to get on your hands and knees facing the handball wall while two people threw the ball at you and tried to nail you in the behind. It hurt, for one, and for another, I never seemed to get my chance to try to nail somebody in the behind. Plus, that day there were my lime-green pants to think about. I didn't want to get dirt smudges on them. "Well?" Harry bounced the ball as though each bounce was a second ticking away. I stared at his stomach, which was always, no matter what, poking out from a shirt that was too small for him.

"I don't want to, Harry."

"Tough titty. We need another person."

"Well, I don't want to get my pants dirty." I kept looking over at Melvin to make sure he was still on the swings across the playground. If recess ended before I got a chance to tell him, he wouldn't have a warning.

"C'mon, man," Harry said. "Quit wasting time." He grabbed the front of my 94.7 KMET T-shirt that I'd gotten from somewhere and wore in hopes I'd have at least one cool piece of clothing. It was one of the radio stations that played Def Leppard and AC/DC, though in secret I still liked my Chi-Lites 45, "Have You Seen Her?" better. Harry started pulling me toward the handball court, and when I resisted, he pulled so hard I fell down. I looked over at the swings. Melvin wasn't there. My slacks had a tear where I fell on my knees. I got mad because I told him to leave me alone and he didn't. I started to cry because I was mad and couldn't kick Harry's ass, couldn't do anything.

"You all right, Av'ry?" Melvin drawled, and suddenly he was standing beside me. I was happy he was there and scared to talk to him, to be caught with Melvin, be a combo with Melvin, permanently paired so nobody would ever accept me because of my connection to Country Cowboy. But I was still in love with his pointy costume ears, and when he spoke my name, it was the first time I'd heard it all day. Not even our teacher, old powdery Mrs. Campbell, had called on me that day. So I mumbled a thanks, I'm OK, and Harry sneered at the both of us just when the freeze bell rang.

It was the bell that told us recess was over and we were to stop whatever it was we were doing, whatever games we were playing, and come back inside. We always took the bell literally. Until the bell stopped ringing, we froze right on the spot, like statues, like mannequins. There were me, Harry, and Melvin, frozen, along with everybody else on the playground, while tetherballs kept twirling and balls kept bouncing.

THIS IS HOW kids start fights: "Hey, so-and-so. I'ma kick your ass." For no reason, out of the blue. So when Melvin was trying to leave school with his jean jacket slung over his shoulder, that's what cross-eyed Eddie said to him. Everybody else just agreed. I had warned Melvin, but all he did was frown and offer me half his piece of Juicy Fruit.

There was, then, the usually core group of fighters and the spectators when Eddie shoved Melvin. "C'mon, Country Cowboy. Fuckin Elvis." Eddie wasn't as tall as Melvin, but he was big and sloppy. Melvin didn't seem concerned, though. He ran his right hand over his crew cut and took his jacket off his shoulder. Melvin didn't want it to get dirty. He handed it to the person closest to him without thinking, gap-toothed John Thompson, who said, "I'm not holding your stupid jacket, Country Ass," and dropped it on the ground. Just for that instant, Melvin looked dumb and awkward, as though he honestly didn't expect such rudeness from anybody. He picked up his jacket and dusted it off. I was behind him and panicked when I thought he might know this, turn around, and ask me to hold his jacket while he fought. What would I do? It had taken me weeks to get to where I was, which wasn't very far, but I was grateful for that slight break in the torture. The tiny thaw in the frost. I was going to Disneyland with Lisa White, and even if she didn't like me so much now, maybe at the party she would see who I really was and then like me.

"Av'ry, hold my jacket, will you?" Melvin held it out and his nostrils flared a little bit when I hesitated. I glanced at Terri, who was looking straight at me with a psychotic grin on her face. Melvin thrust the jacket at me. I took it. And then, well, it slipped from my fingers and fell to the ground. Melvin looked at his jacket and then at me, those pale blue eyes looking at me brand new and different from any time before. We both left the jacket there, and then he beat the shit out of Harry, then Hector, then Eddie. Not Terri, because she was a girl, but she chased me home for two weeks straight, even though I didn't hold the jacket, and even though Melvin didn't care when I told him that they were going to kick his ass after school.

WALKING HOME AFTER the fight, Melvin didn't say more than five words to me. I can't even say that he walked home *with* me, because he was walking fast and I couldn't keep up. His legs were so long, and for every stride he took I had to take two. I was looking forward to him searching for his cigarettes in the ivy, but he said he wasn't going to go the way we usually went. He was going home another way. I couldn't blame him for being disappointed in me, I'd let him down after he'd come to my rescue during recess. But couldn't he understand that, really and truly, it wasn't a personal thing. Couldn't he understand that I could be completely in love with him, but just not want to make waves? And anyway, it wasn't like I *threw* the jacket down or anything. It slipped.

"But, Melvin," I said, trying to get him to go my way. "This is the quickest way to get home. Your house is straight ahead. Plus, what about your cigarettes? Aren't you dying for a cigarette?"

"Darlin . . ." He pulled a cigarette from his jacket pocket and put it behind his ear. "I can get by with what I got right here until later."

Darlin. I'd never heard that from him, calling me that before. I didn't like the way it felt, like a pat on the head. Not like when he said my name, which felt like a kiss.

"See ya round," Melvin said and turned, walking uphill. I watched him for as long as I could see him, and I still didn't know that he was never going to walk my way again, but I was thinking, *You probably should have picked up his jacket. Pro-ba-bly.*

Too late. Melvin got farther and farther away, MEL on the back of his jacket, shimmering like diamonds, like he was some superstar. And me, I was feeling as though I wished somebody fighting had slugged me, too.

I WALKED UP the hill to my house and replayed Melvin's fight. Only in my mind, it wasn't Melvin's fight. It became my fight. I imagined I had on a bad outfit, windowpane pants and a leather jacket, new—not used—and a large, perfectly round Afro like the one Foxy Brown had when she pulled a gun from it and blew away some white man who was messing with her. Owen was obsessed with Pam Grier and her big breasts, and I was awed by her ability to whup ass. People who messed with Foxy were sorry, all right. Just when they thought she was all brown sugar in a halter top, she had a gun or a karate kick to set them straight.

Listen, I said. I was talking to myself. *All y'all mothafuckas better leave Melvin alone. That's right, I cussed. And I did say, mutha-fucka, not mo-ther fuck-er. It's the way I speak, dumb-asses, and unless you want your butt kicked, you best to leave me and my man alone. Who you calling a nigga?* I swung around and pointed a gun at the nearest palm tree. *That's what I thought.*

I kept replaying my and Melvin's fight. When I got in the house, I was surprised to see Owen at the refrigerator, home from work early, drinking milk from a carton.

"You not supposed to be doing that. Mama said."

"Mama said," he mimicked me. "You always got to do everything everybody say, goody-goody. Who were you talking to, anyway?"

I put my books down on the dining room table, round and glass. I didn't want to stop my daydream. Melvin was holding my hand. *Darlin, I guess you told them what side of the sidewalk they can spit on, didn't you?*

I went to the cabinet for a glass and poured myself a glass of milk dramatically, to show Owen how it was supposed to be done. He thumped me on the head.

"You still ain't told me who you was talking to all loud."

I drank my milk down in two gulps, washed my glass out then and there because Mama liked her kitchen kept neat, and then I picked up my books so I could go to my room and get out of my torn green pants. "Nobody. OK? I wasn't saying anything to anybody. I was just talking to myself."

"Trippin," he said, making his way to his room. He hardly seemed fazed by anything, not even moving to the suburbs.

"Hey," I said. "Owen."

"What?"

"Isn't it weird going to school with all these white people sometime? Don't it make you feel . . ." My voice trailed off. I was looking for the word. "Bad? *Doesn't* it make you feel bad?"

"What?" Owen rolled his eyes. "I'm graduating this year, Ave.

I ain't stuttin these white folks." He went into his room and closed the door and soon I could hear Peabo Bryson blaring from his stereo, *I'm so into you, I don't know what I'm gonna do.*

Stuttin, Owen said. Stuttin meant "studying." I repeated the word in my head. I'd heard that word my whole life from my grandmamas, Mama, Daddy, everybody. But when Owen said it then, "stuttin" sounded like a word he'd just made up. For the first time I really heard what the kids in school heard when I spoke. Owen sounded strange to me, from someplace else, using that word. Part of a language I knew but was already beginning to forget.

DISCUSSION QUESTIONS

1. "And of course I was. All eleven-year-olds were. I was out of my mind, especially for Melvin. Couldn't anybody understand that if I had just one cool outfit, like Melvin, I'd be on my way to the kids liking me for reals?" Do you think the narrator really loves Melvin? How does Johnson evoke her longing?

2. What do you make of the narrator's reactions to Terri's cruel insults? What do you make of Avery's unexpected rejection of Melvin?

3. What role does language play in this story? Discuss the closing lines of the short story: "Owen sounded strange to me, from someplace else, using that word. Part of a language I knew but was already beginning to forget." What is the narrator beginning to learn about herself and her new environment?

Everyday Use

Alice Walker

Originally published in 1973

Dee wanted nice things. A yellow organdy dress to
wear to her graduation from high school; black pumps
to match a green suit she'd made from an old suit
somebody gave me. She was determined to stare down
any disaster in her efforts.

I will wait for her in the yard that Maggie and I made so clean
and wavy yesterday afternoon. A yard like this is more comfortable than most people know. It is not just a yard. It is like
an extended living room. When the hard clay is swept clean as a
floor and the fine sand around the edges lined with tiny, irregu-
lar grooves, anyone can come and sit and look up into the elm
tree and wait for the breezes that never come inside the house.

Maggie will be nervous until after her sister goes: she will
stand hopelessly in corners, homely and ashamed of the burn
scars down her arms and legs, eyeing her sister with a mixture
of envy and awe. She thinks her sister has held life always in the

palm of one hand, that "no" is a word the world never learned to say to her.

You've no doubt seen those TV shows where the child who has "made it" is confronted, as a surprise, by her own mother and father, tottering in weakly from backstage. (A pleasant surprise, of course: What would they do if parent and child came on the show only to curse out and insult each other?) On TV mother and child embrace and smile into each other's faces. Sometimes the mother and father weep, the child wraps them in her arms and leans across the table to tell how she would not have made it without their help. I have seen these programs.

Sometimes I dream a dream in which Dee and I are suddenly brought together on a TV program of this sort. Out of a dark and soft-seated limousine I am ushered into a bright room filled with many people. There I meet a smiling, gray, sporty man like Johnny Carson who shakes my hand and tells me what a fine girl I have. Then we are on the stage and Dee is embracing me with tears in her eyes. She pins on my dress a large orchid, even though she has told me once that she thinks orchids are tacky flowers.

In real life I am a large, big-boned woman with rough, man-working hands. In the winter I wear flannel nightgowns to bed and overalls during the day. I can kill and clean a hog as mercilessly as a man. My fat keeps me hot in zero weather. I can work outside all day, breaking ice to get water for washing; I can eat pork liver cooked over the open fire minutes after it comes steaming from the hog. One winter I knocked a bull calf straight in the brain between the eyes with a sledgehammer and had the meat hung up to chill before nightfall. But of course all this does not show on television. I am the way my daughter would want me to be: a hundred pounds lighter, my skin like an uncooked barley pancake. My hair glistens in the hot bright lights. Johnny Carson has much to do to keep up with my quick and witty tongue.

But that is a mistake. I know even before I wake up. Who ever knew a Johnson with a quick tongue? Who can even imagine me looking a strange white man in the eye? It seems to me I have talked to them always with one foot raised in flight, with my head fumed in whichever way is farthest from them. Dee, though. She would always look anyone in the eye. Hesitation was no part of her nature.

"HOW DO I LOOK, MAMA?" Maggie says, showing just enough of her thin body enveloped in pink skirt and red blouse for me to know she's there, almost hidden by the door.

"Come out into the yard," I say.

Have you ever seen a lame animal, perhaps a dog run over by some careless person rich enough to own a car, sidle up to someone who is ignorant enough to be kind to him? That is the way my Maggie walks. She has been like this, chin on chest, eyes on ground, feet in shuffle, ever since the fire that burned the other house to the ground.

Dee is lighter than Maggie, with nicer hair and a fuller figure. She's a woman now, though sometimes I forget. How long ago was it that the other house burned? Ten, twelve years? Sometimes I can still hear the flames and feel Maggie's arms sticking to me, her hair smoking and her dress falling off her in little black papery flakes. Her eyes seemed stretched open, blazed open by the flames reflected in them. And Dee. I see her standing off under the sweet gum tree she used to dig gum out of; a look of concentration on her face as she watched the last dingy gray board of the house fall in toward the red-hot brick chimney. Why don't you do a dance around the ashes? I'd wanted to ask her. She had hated the house that much.

I used to think she hated Maggie too. But that was before we raised money, the church and me, to send her to Augusta to school. She used to read to us without pity; forcing words, lies, other folks' habits, whole lives upon us two, sitting trapped and ignorant underneath her voice. She washed us in a river of make-believe, burned us with a lot of knowledge we didn't necessarily need to know. Pressed us to her with the serious way she read, to shove us away, like dimwits, at just the moment we seemed about to understand.

Dee wanted nice things. A yellow organdy dress to wear to her graduation from high school; black pumps to match a green suit she'd made from an old suit somebody gave me. She was determined to stare down any disaster in her efforts. Her eyelids would not flicker for minutes at a time. Often I fought off the temptation to shake her. At sixteen she had a style of her own: and knew what style was.

I never had an education myself. After second grade the school was closed down. Don't ask me why: in 1927 colored asked fewer questions than they do now. Sometimes Maggie reads to me. She stumbles along good-naturedly but can't see well. She knows she is not bright. Like good looks and money, quickness passes her by. She will marry John Thomas (who has mossy teeth in an earnest face) and then I'll be free to sit here and I guess just sing church songs to myself. Although I never was a good singer. Never could carry a tune. I was always better at a man's job. I used to love to milk till I was hooked in the side in '49. Cows are soothing and slow and don't bother you, unless you try to milk them the wrong way.

I have deliberately turned my back on the house. It is three rooms, just like the one that burned, except the roof is tin; they don't make shingle roofs anymore. There are no real windows, just some holes cut in the sides, like the portholes in a ship, but not round and not square, with rawhide holding the shutters up on the outside. This house is in a pasture too, like the other one. No doubt when Dee sees it she will want to tear it down. She wrote me once that no matter where we "choose" to live, she will manage to come see us. But she will never bring her friends. Maggie and I thought about this and Maggie asked me, "Mama, when did Dee ever *have* any friends?"

She had a few. Furtive boys in pink shirts hanging about on washday after school. Nervous girls who never laughed. Impressed with her, they worshiped the well-turned phrase, the cute shape, the scalding humor that erupted like bubbles in lye. She read to them.

When she was courting Jimmy T she didn't have much time to pay to us, but turned all her fault-finding power on him. He *flew* to marry a cheap city girl from a family of ignorant flashy people. She hardly had time to recompose herself.

WHEN SHE COMES I will meet . . . but there they are!

Maggie attempts to make a dash for the house, in her shuffling way, but I stay her with my hand. "Come back here," I say. And she stops and tries to dig a well in the sand with her toe.

It is hard to see them clearly through the strong sun. But

even the first glimpse of leg out of the car tells me it is Dee. Her feet were always neat looking, as if God himself had shaped them with a certain style. From the other side of the car comes a short, stocky man. Hair is all over his head a foot long and hanging from his chin like a kinky mule tail. I hear Maggie suck in her breath. "Uhnnnh," is what it sounds like. Like when you see the wriggling end of a snake just in front of your foot on the road. "Uhnnnh."

Dee next. A dress down to the ground, in this hot weather. A dress so loud it hurts my eyes. There are yellows and oranges enough to throw back the light of the sun. I feel my whole face warming from the heat waves it throws out. Earrings gold, too, and hanging down to her shoulders. Bracelets dangling and making noises when she moves her arm up to shake the folds of the dress out of her armpits. The dress is loose and flows, and as she walks closer, I like it. I hear Maggie go "Uhnnnh" again. It is her sister's hair. It stands straight up like the wool on a sheep. It is black as night and around the edges are two long pigtails that rope about like small lizards disappearing behind her ears.

"Wa-su-zo-Tean-o!" she says, coming on in that gliding way the dress makes her move. The short stocky fellow with the hair to his navel is all grinning and he follows up with "Asalamala-kim, my mother and sister!" He moves to hug Maggie but she falls back, right up against the back of my chair. I feel her trembling there and when I look up I see the perspiration falling off her chin.

"Don't get up," says Dee. Since I am stout it takes something of a push. You can see me trying to move a second or two before I make it. She turns, showing white heels through her sandals, and goes back to the car. Out she peeks next with a Polaroid. She

stoops down quickly and snaps off picture after picture of me
sitting there in front of the house with Maggie cowering behind
me. She never takes a shot without making sure the house is
included. When a cow comes nibbling around the edge of the
yard she snaps it and me and Maggie *and* the house. Then she
puts the Polaroid in the back seat of the car, and comes up and
kisses me on the forehead.

Meanwhile Asalamalakim is going through motions with
Maggie's hand. Maggie's hand is as limp as a fish, and probably
as cold, despite the sweat, and she keeps trying to pull it back. It
looks like Asalamalakim wants to shake hands but wants to do
it fancy. Or maybe he don't know how people shake hands. Any-
how, he soon gives up on Maggie.

"Well," I say. "Dee."

"No, Mama," she says. "Not 'Dee,' Wangero Leewanika
Kemanjo!"

"What happened to 'Dee'?" I wanted to know.

"She's dead," Wangero said. "I couldn't bear it any longer,
being named after the people who oppress me."

"You know as well as me you was named after your aunt
Dicie," I said. Dicie is my sister. She named Dee. We called her
"Big Dee" after Dee was born.

"But who was *she* named after?" asked Wangero.

"I guess after Grandma Dee," I said.

"And who was she named after?" asked Wangero.

"Her mother," I said, and saw Wangero was getting tired.
"That's about as far back as I can trace it," I said. Though, in
fact, I probably could have carried it back beyond the Civil War
through the branches.

"Well," said Asalamalakim, "there you are."

"Uhnnnh," I heard Maggie say.

"There I was not," I said, "before 'Dicie' cropped up in our family, so why should I try to trace it that far back?"

He just stood there grinning, looking down on me like somebody inspecting a Model A car. Every once in a while he and Wangero sent eye signals over my head.

"How do you pronounce this name?" I asked.

"You don't have to call me by it if you don't want to," said Wangero.

"Why shouldn't I?" I asked. "If that's what you want us to call you, we'll call you."

"I know it might sound awkward at first," said Wangero.

"I'll get used to it," I said. "Ream it out again."

Well, soon we got the name out of the way. Asalamalakim had a name twice as long and three times as hard. After I tripped over it two or three times he told me to just call him Hakim-a-barber. I wanted to ask him was he a barber, but I didn't really think he was, so I didn't ask.

"You must belong to those beef cattle peoples down the road," I said. They said "Asalamalakim" when they met you, too, but they didn't shake hands. Always too busy: feeding the cattle, fixing the fences, putting up salt-lick shelters, throwing down hay. When the white folks poisoned some of the herd, the men stayed up all night with rifles in their hands. I walked a mile and a half just to see the sight.

Hakim-a-barber said, "I accept some of their doctrines, but farming and raising cattle is not my style." They didn't tell me, and I didn't ask, whether Wangero (Dee) had really gone and married him.

We sat down to eat and right away he said he didn't eat

collards and pork was unclean. Wangero, though, went on through the chitlins and corn bread, the greens and everything else. She talked a blue streak over the sweet potatoes. Everything delighted her. Even the fact that we still used the benches her daddy made for the table when we couldn't afford to buy chairs.

"Oh, Mama!" she cried. Then turned to Hakim-a-barber. "I never knew how lovely these benches are. You can feel the rump prints," she said, running her hands underneath her and along the bench. Then she gave a sigh and her hand closed over Grandma Dee's butter dish. "That's it!" she said. "I knew there was something I wanted to ask you if I could have." She jumped up from the table and went over in the corner where the churn stood, the milk in it clabber by now. She looked at the churn and looked at it.

"This churn top is what I need," she said. "Didn't Uncle Buddy whittle it out of a tree you all used to have?"

"Yes," I said.

"Uh huh," she said happily. "And I want the dasher, too."

"Uncle Buddy whittle that, too?" asked the barber.

Dee (Wangero) looked up at me.

"Aunt Dee's first husband whittled the dash," said Maggie so low you almost couldn't hear her. "His name was Henry, but they called him Stash."

"Maggie's brain is like an elephant's," Wangero said, laughing. "I can use the churn top as a centerpiece for the alcove table," she said, sliding a plate over the churn, "and I'll think of something artistic to do with the dasher."

When she finished wrapping the dasher the handle stuck out. I took it for a moment in my hands. You didn't even have to look close to see where hands pushing the dasher up and down to make butter had left a kind of sink in the wood. In fact, there were a lot of small sinks; you could see where thumbs and fingers had sunk into the wood. It was beautiful light yellow wood, from a tree that grew in the yard where Big Dee and Stash had lived.

After dinner Dee (Wangero) went to the trunk at the foot of my bed and started rifling through it. Maggie hung back in the kitchen over the dishpan. Out came Wangero with two quilts. They had been pieced by Grandma Dee and then Big Dee and me had hung them on the quilt frames on the front porch and quilted them. One was in the Lone Star pattern. The other was Walk Around the Mountain. In both of them were scraps of dresses Grandma Dee had worn fifty and more years ago. Bits and pieces of Grandpa Jarrell's paisley shirts. And one teeny faded blue piece, about the size of a penny matchbox, that was from Great Grandpa Ezra's uniform that he wore in the Civil War.

"Mama," Wangero said sweet as a bird. "Can I have these old quilts?"

I heard something fall in the kitchen, and a minute later the kitchen door slammed.

"Why don't you take one or two of the others?" I asked. "These old things was just done by me and Big Dee from some tops your grandma pieced before she died."

"No," said Wangero. "I don't want those. They are stitched around the borders by machine."

"That'll make them last better," I said.

"That's not the point," said Wangero. "These are all pieces of dresses Grandma used to wear. She did all this stitching by hand. Imagine!" She held the quilts securely in her arms, stroking them.

"Some of the pieces, like those lavender ones, come from old clothes her mother handed down to her," I said, moving up to touch the quilts. Dee (Wangero) moved back just enough so that I couldn't reach the quilts. They already belonged to her.

"Imagine!" she breathed again, clutching them closely to her bosom.

"The truth is," I said, "I promised to give them quilts to Maggie, for when she marries John Thomas."

She gasped like a bee had stung her.

"Maggie can't appreciate these quilts!" she said. "She'd probably be backward enough to put them to everyday use."

"I reckon she would," I said. "God knows I been saving 'em for long enough with nobody using 'em. I hope she will!" I didn't want to bring up how I had offered Dee (Wangero) a quilt when she went away to college. Then she had told they were old-fashioned, out of style.

"But they're *priceless*!" she was saying now, furiously; for she has a temper. "Maggie would put them on the bed and in five years they'd be in rags. Less than that!"

"She can always make some more," I said. "Maggie knows how to quilt."

Dee (Wangero) looked at me with hatred. "You just will not understand. The point is these quilts, *these* quilts!"

"Well," I said, stumped. "What would *you* do with them?"

"Hang them," she said. As if that was the only thing you *could* do with quilts.

MAGGIE BY NOW was standing in the door. I could almost hear the sound her feet made as they scraped over each other.

"She can have them, Mama," she said, like somebody used to

never winning anything, or having anything reserved for her. "I can 'member Grandma Dee without the quilts."

I looked at her hard. She had filled her bottom lip with checkerberry snuff and gave her face a kind of dopey, hangdog look. It was Grandma Dee and Big Dee who taught her how to quilt herself. She stood there with her scarred hands hidden in the folds of her skirt. She looked at her sister with something like fear but she wasn't mad at her. This was Maggie's portion. This was the way she knew God to work.

When I looked at her like that something hit me in the top of my head and ran down to the soles of my feet. Just like when I'm in church and the spirit of God touches me and I get happy and shout. I did something I never done before: hugged Maggie to me, then dragged her on into the room, snatched the quilts out of Miss Wangero's hands and dumped them into Maggie's lap. Maggie just sat there on my bed with her mouth open.

"Take one or two of the others," I said to Dee.

But she turned without a word and went out to Hakim-a-barber.

"YOU JUST DON'T UNDERSTAND," she said, as Maggie and I came out to the car.

"What don't I understand?" I wanted to know.

"Your heritage," she said. And then she turned to Maggie, kissed her, and said, "You ought to try to make something of yourself too, Maggie. It's really a new day for us. But from the way you and Mama still live you'd never know it."

She put on some sunglasses that hid everything above the tip of her nose and chin.

Maggie smiled; maybe at the sunglasses. But a real smile, not scared. After we watched the car dust settle I asked Maggie to bring me a dip of snuff. And then the two of us sat there just enjoying, until it was time to go in the house and go to bed.

DISCUSSION QUESTIONS

1. Discuss Dee's mother and sister. How have her relationships with them influenced what she expects from the people in her life? How have they shaped her view of herself as an individual?

2. Compare and contrast the sisters. Why do you think they turned out so differently? In what ways are they similar to their mother?

3. How is love portrayed in this story? By the end of the story, are there unspoken rules that shift the dynamic between the mother and her two daughters?

4. How do you interpret the story's title?

We're the Only Colored People Here

Gwendolyn Brooks

Originally published in 1953

Though she knew that once the spell was over it would be a year, two years, more, before he would return to the World Playhouse. And he might never go to a real play. But she was learning to love moments. To love moments for themselves.

When they went out to the car there were just the very finest bits of white powder coming down, with an almost comical little ethereal hauteur, to add themselves to the really important, piled-up masses of their kind.

And it wasn't cold.

Maud Martha laughed happily to herself. It was pleasant out, and tonight she and Paul were very close to each other.

He held the door open for her—instead of going on round to the driving side, getting in, and leaving her to get in at her side as best she might. When he took this way of calling her "lady" and

informing her of his love she felt precious, protected, delicious.
She gave him an excited look of gratitude. He smiled indulgently.

"Want it to be the Owl again?"

"Oh, no, no, Paul. Let's not go there tonight. I feel too good
inside for that. Let's go downtown?"

She had to suggest that with a question mark at the end,
always. He usually had three protests. Too hard to park. Too
much money. Too many white folks. And tonight she could
almost certainly expect a no, she feared, because he had come
out in his blue work shirt. There was a spot of apricot juice on the
collar, too. His shoes were not shined.

... But he nodded!

"We've never been to the World Playhouse," she said cautiously. "They have a good picture. I'd feel rich in there."

"You really wanta?"

"Please?"

"Sure."

It wasn't like other movie houses. People from the Studebaker
Theatre which, as Maud Martha whispered to Paul, was "all-
locked-arms" with the World Playhouse, were strolling up and
down the lobby, laughing softly, smoking with gentle grace.

"There must be a play going on in there and this is probably an
intermission," Maud Martha whispered again.

"I don't know why you feel you got to whisper," whispered
Paul. "Nobody else is whispering in here." He looked around,
resentfully, wanting to see a few, just a few colored faces. There
were only their own.

Maud Martha laughed a nervous defiant little laugh; and
spoke loudly. "There certainly isn't any reason to whisper. Silly,
huh."

WE'RE THE ONLY COLORED PEOPLE HERE

The strolling women were cleverly gowned. Some of them had flowers or flashers in their hair. They looked—cooked. Well cared-for. And as though they had never seen a roach or a rat in their lives. Or gone without heat for a week. And the men had even edges. They were men, Maud Martha thought, who wouldn't stoop to fret over less than a thousand dollars.

"We're the only colored people here," said Paul.

She hated him a little. "Oh, hell. Who in hell cares."

"Well, what I want to know is, where do you pay the damn fares."

"There's the box office. Go on up."

He went on up. It was closed.

"Well," sighed Maud Martha, "I guess the picture has started already. But we can't have missed much. Go on up to that girl at the candy counter and ask her where we should pay our money."

He didn't want to do that. The girl was lovely and blonde and cold-eyed, and her arms were akimbo, and the set of her head was eloquent. No one else was at the counter.

"Well. We'll wait a minute. And see—"

Maud Martha hated him again. Coward. She ought to flounce over to the girl herself—show him up. . . .

The people in the lobby tried to avoid looking curiously at two shy Negroes wanting desperately not to seem shy. The white women looked at the Negro woman in her outfit with which no special fault could be found, but which made them think, somehow, of close rooms, and wee, close lives. They looked at her hair. They were always slightly surprised, but agreeably so, when they did. They supposed it was the hair that had got her that yellowish, good-looking Negro man without a tie.

An usher opened a door of the World Playhouse part and ran

quickly down the few steps that led from it to the lobby. Paul opened his mouth.

"Say, fella. Where do we get the tickets for the movie?"

The usher glanced at Paul's feet before answering. Then he said coolly, but not unpleasantly, "I'll take the money."

They were able to go in.

And the picture! Maud Martha was so glad that they had not gone to the Owl! Here was technicolor, and the love story was sweet. And there was classical music that silvered its way into you and made your back cold. And the theater itself! It was no palace, no such Great Shakes as the Tivoli out south, for instance (where many colored people went every night). But you felt good sitting there, yes, good, and as if when you left it you would be going home to a sweet-smelling apartment with flowers on little gleaming tables; and wonderful silver on night-blue velvet, in chests; and crackly sheets; and lace spreads on such beds as you saw at Marshall Field's. Instead of back to your kit'u't apt., with the garbage of your floor's families in a big can just outside your door, and the gray sound of little gray feet scratching away from it as you drag up those flights of narrow complaining stairs.

Paul pressed her hand. Paul said, "We oughta do this more often."

And again. "We'll have to do this more often. And go to plays, too. I mean at that Blackstone, and Studebaker."

She pressed back, smiling beautifully to herself in the darkness. Though she knew that once the spell was over it would be a year, two years, more, before he would return to the World Playhouse. And he might never go to a real play. But she was learning to love moments. To love moments for themselves.

When the picture was over, and the lights revealed them for

what they were, the Negroes stood up among the furs and good cloth and faint perfume, looked about them eagerly. They hoped they would meet no cruel eyes. They hoped no one would look intruded upon. They had enjoyed the picture so they were so happy, they wanted to laugh, to say warmly to the other outgoers, "Good, huh? Wasn't it swell?"

This, of course, they could not do. But if only no one would look intruded upon. . . .

DISCUSSION QUESTIONS

1. This story is a vignette from Brooks's novel *Maud Martha*, which follows a girl from childhood to adulthood in Chicago. Though the title character is an adult in this story, there's a youthfulness to her. How do you interpret her relationship with Paul? With herself?

2. What does the movie theater represent for Maud Martha? For Paul?

3. At the end of the story, Brooks writes, "But she was learning to love moments." What does this mean in the context of the story? In what ways are the "moments" valuable in one's life?

Self-Discovery

Seeing Things Simply

Edwidge Danticat

Originally published in 2012

This is why she wanted to make pictures, to have something to leave behind even after she was gone, something that showed what she had observed in a way that no one else had and no one else would after her.

"Get it! Kill it!"

The cockfight had just begun. Princesse heard the shouting from the school yard as she came out of class. The rooster that crowed the loudest usually received the first blow. It was often the first to die.

The cheers burst into a roar. As Princesse crossed the dusty road, she could hear the men shouting. "Take its head off! Go for its throat!"

At night, *vodou* ceremonies were held around the shady banyan tree that rose from the middle of an open hut. However, during the days the villagers held animal fights there, and sometimes even weddings and funerals. Outside the fight ring, a few women sold iced drinks and tickets to the Dominican lottery.

There was an old man in front of the yard smoking a badly carved wooden pipe.

"Let's go home," his wife was saying to him as she balanced a heavy basket on her head.

"Let me be or I'll make you hush," he shouted at her.

He dug his foot deep into the brown dusty grass to put a spell on her that would make her mute.

The wife threw her head back all the way, so far that you could have cut her throat and she wouldn't have felt it. She laughed like she was chortling at the clouds and walked away.

The man blew his pipe smoke in his wife's direction. He continued to push his foot deep into the grass, cursing his wife as she went on her way, the basket swaying from side to side on her head.

"What a pretty girl you are." The old man winked as Princesse approached him. The closer Princesse came, the more clearly she could see his face. He was a former schoolteacher from the capital who had moved to Ville Rose, as far as anyone could tell, to get drunk.

The old man was handsome in an odd kind of way, with a gray streak running through the middle of his hair. He sat outside of the cockfights every day, listening as though it were a kind of music, shooing away his wife with spells that never worked.

There was talk in the village that he was a very educated man, had studied at the Sorbonne in Paris, France. The word was that such a man would only live with a woman who carried a basket on her head because he himself had taken a big fall in the world. He might be running from the law, or maybe a charm had been placed on him, which would explain why every ordinary hex he tried to put on his wife failed to work.

"How are you today?" he asked, reaching for the hem of Princesse's dress. Princesse was sixteen but because she was very short and thin could easily pass for twelve. "Do you want to place a wager on the roosters?" he asked her jokingly.

"No sir," she said as she continued on her way.

The old man took a gulp from a bottle filled with rum and leaves and limped towards the yard where the fight was taking place.

The roosters were whimpering. The battle was near its end. There was another loud burst of cheers, this one longer than the last. It was the sound of a cheerful death. One of the roosters had lost the fight.

PRINCESSE WAS ON HER WAY to keep an appointment with Catherine, a painter from Guadeloupe. A row of houses in Ville Rose was occupied by a group of foreigners. Princesse had met a few of them through the teachers at her school. The students in her class were rewarded for good grades by being introduced to the French-speaking artists and writers who lived in the gingerbread houses perched on the hills that overlooked Ville Rose's white sand beaches.

Catherine was reading on the beach when Princesse called down to her from the hill.

"Madame," Princesse said, calling upon her phonetics lessons in order to sound less native and more French.

Catherine put down her book and threw a thigh-length robe over her bathing suit as she ran up to the house. There, she kissed Princesse on both cheeks as though they were meeting at a party.

Catherine was only twenty-seven years old but looked much

older. She sunbathed endlessly, but her skin stayed the same copper-tinged shade, even as it became more and more dried out. Of any black person that Princesse knew, Catherine spent the most time in the sun without changing color.

Catherine already had her canvas and paint set up on the veranda of her house. She liked to paint outdoors in the sun.

"Relax, *chérie*," she assured Princesse. "Just take your own time to become comfortable. Heaven and earth will be here long after we're gone. We're in no rush."

Princesse slowly removed the checkered blouse of her school uniform, followed by a spotless white undershirt she wore to keep her blouse from getting stained with sweat. She had breasts like mushrooms, big ones that just hadn't spread yet.

Catherine began to sketch as Princesse took off her skirt. It was always hardest getting Princesse to remove her panties, but once Catherine either turned around or pretended to close her eyes, they were gone in a flash.

"Now we work," Catherine said to Princesse as the girl reclined on a white sheet that Catherine had laid out for her on the floor of the veranda. Princesse liked to sit beneath the rail of the veranda, hidden from the view of any passersby.

One day Catherine hoped to get Princesse to roam naked on the beach attempting to make love to the crest of an ocean wave, but for now it was enough for her to make Princesse comfortable with her nudity while safely hidden from the sight of onlookers.

"It's not so bad," Catherine said, making quick pencil strokes on the sketch pad in her hand to delineate Princesse's naked breasts. "Relax. Pretend that you're in your bed alone and very comfortable."

It was hard for Princesse to pretend with ease as the sun beamed into her private parts.

"Remember what I've told you," Catherine said. "I will never use your name and no one who lives in this village will ever see these paintings."

Princesse relaxed in the glow of this promise.

"One day your grandchildren will walk into galleries in France," Catherine said, "and *there* they'll admire your beautiful body."

There was nothing so beautiful about her body, Princesse thought. She had a body like all the others who lived here except she was willing to be naked. But after she was dead and buried, she wouldn't care who saw her body. It would be up to Catherine and God to decide that. As long as Catherine never showed anyone in Ville Rose the portraits, she would be content.

Catherine never displayed any intention of sharing her work with Princesse. After she felt that she had painted enough of them, Catherine would pack up her canvases and bring them to either Paris or to Guadeloupe for safekeeping.

Catherine stopped sketching for a second to get herself a glass of iced rum. She offered some to Princesse, who shook her head, no. The village would surely smell the rum on her breath when she returned home and would conjecture quickly as to where she had gotten it.

"I used to pose for classes when I was in France." Catherine leaned back on the rail of the veranda and slowly sipped. "I posed for art students in Paris. That's how I made my living for a while."

"How was it?" Princesse asked, her eyes closed against the glare of the sun as it bounced off the glass of clear white rum in Catherine's hand.

"It was very difficult for me," Catherine answered, "just as it is for you. The human form in all its complexity is not the easiest thing to re-create. It is hard to catch a likeness of a person unless the artist knows the person very well. That's why, once you find someone whose likeness you've mastered, it's hard to let them go."

Catherine picked up the pad once more. Princesse lay back and said nothing. A wandering fly parked itself on her nose. She smacked it away. A streak of coconut pomade melting in Princesse's hair fell onto the white sheet stretched out on the veranda floor beneath her. The grease made a stain on the mat like the spots her period often made in the back of her dresses.

"No two faces are ever the same," Catherine said, her wrist moving quickly back and forth across the pad. The pencil made a slight sweeping noise as though it were grating down the finer, more resistant surfaces of the white page. "The eyes are the most striking and astonishing aspects of the face."

"What about the mouth?" Princesse asked.

"That is very crucial too, my dear, because the lips determine the expression of the face."

Princesse pulled her lips together in an exaggerated pout.

"You mean like that?" she asked, giggling.

"Exactly," Catherine said.

CATHERINE FLIPPED the cover of her pad when she was done.

"You can go now, Princesse," she said.

Princesse dressed quickly. Catherine squeezed two gourdes between her palms, kissing her twice on the cheek.

Princesse rushed down the steps leading away from the beach house. She kept walking until she reached the hard dirt road that stretched back to the village.

IT WAS NIGHTFALL. In a cloud of dust, an old jeep clattered down the road.

Someone was playing a drum in the fight yard. The calls of conch shells and hollow cow horns were attempting to catch up to the insistent rhythm.

A man wept as he buried his rooster, which had died in one of the fights that afternoon. "Ayïbobo," the man said, chanting to the stars as he dropped the bird into a small hole that he had dug along the side of the road. One of the stars answered by plunging down from the sky, landing in a fiery ball behind a hill.

"You could have eaten that rooster!" the old drunk hollered at him. "I'm going to come and get that bird tonight and eat it with my wife on Sunday. What a waste!"

"I am giving it back to my father!" hollered back the distressed man. "He gave me this bird last year."

"Your father is dead, you fool!" cried the old drunk.

"I am giving this bird back to him."

The old man was still sitting by the fence cradling his leaf-crammed bottle of rum.

"My great luck, twice in a day, I get to see you," he said to Princesse as she walked by.

"Twice in a day," Princesse agreed, the wind blowing through her skirt.

The human body is an extremely complex form. So Princesse

was learning. A good painting would not only capture the old man's features but also his moods and personality. This could be done with a lot of fancy brushstrokes or with one single flirting line, all depending on the skill of the artist. Each time she went to Catherine's, Princesse would learn something different.

THE NEXT DAY, Catherine had her sit fully clothed on a rock on the beach as she painted her on canvas. Princesse watched her own skin grow visibly darker as she sat near the open sea, the waves spraying a foam of white sand onto her toes.

"In the beginning God said, 'Let there be light.'" Catherine's brush attacked the canvas as she spoke, quickly mixing burnished colors to catch the harsh afternoon light. "Without light, there is nothing. We might as well be blind people. No light or colors."

For the moment, Catherine was painting the rock and the sand beneath Princesse, ignoring the main subject. She was waiting for just the right moment to add Princesse to the canvas. She might even do it later, after the sun had set, when she could paint at her leisure. She might do it the next day when the light would have changed slightly, when the sun was just a little higher or lower in the sky, turning the sea a different shade.

"It's dazzling how the light filters through your complexion," Catherine assured Princesse. "They say black absorbs all color. It blots and consumes it and gives us nothing back. That's wrong, don't you think?"

"Of course," Princesse nodded. Catherine was the expert. She was always right.

"Black skin gives so much to the canvas," Catherine continued.

"Do you ever think of how we change things and how they change us?"

"How?" ventured Princesse.

"Perhaps the smaller things—like human beings, for example— can also change and affect the bigger things in the universe."

A FEW DAYS LATER, Princesse sat in Catherine's bedroom as Catherine sketched her seated in a rocking chair holding a tall red candle in each hand. Black drapes on the window kept out the light of the afternoon sky. A small mole of melted candle wax grew on Princesse's hand as she sat posing stiffly.

"When I was just beginning to paint in Paris," Catherine told Princesse in the dark, "I used to live with a man who was already an artist. He told me that if I wanted to be an artist, I would have to wear boots, a pair of his large clunky boots with holes in the soles. That man was my best teacher. He died yesterday."

"I am sorry," Princesse said, seeing no real strain of loss in Catherine's eyes.

"It's fine," Catherine said. "He was old and sickly."

"What was it like, wearing those shoes?" Princesse asked.

"I see where your interests lie," Catherine said.

"I am sorry if that was insensitive."

"I would tell him to go somewhere and perform obscene acts on himself every time he told me to wear the boots," Catherine said, "but whenever he went on a trip, I would make myself live in those shoes. I wore them every day, everywhere I went. I would wear them on the street, in the park, to the butcher's. I wore them everywhere I could until they felt like mine for a while."

THE NEXT DAY when Princesse went to see Catherine, she did not paint her. Instead they sat on the veranda while Catherine drank white rum.

"Let me hear you talk," Catherine said. "Tell me, what color do you think the sky is right now?"

Princesse looked up and saw a color typical of the Haitian sky.

"I guess it's blue," Princesse said. "Indigo, maybe, like the kind we use in the wash."

"We have so much here," Catherine said. "Even wash indigo in the sky."

CATHERINE WAS NOT HOME when Princesse came the next afternoon. Princesse waited outside on the beach-house steps until it was almost nightfall. Finally, Princesse walked down to the beach and watched the stars line up in random battalions in the evening sky.

There was a point in the far distance where the sky almost seemed to blend with the sea, stroking the surface the way two people's lips would touch each other's.

Standing there, Princesse wished she could paint that. That and all the night skies that she had seen, the full moon and the stars peeking down like tiny gods acting out their will, plunging and sometimes winking in a tease, in a parade ignored by humankind. Princesse thought that she could paint that, giving it light and color, shape and texture, all those things that Catherine spoke of.

PRINCESSE RETURNED the following day to find Catherine still absent. She walked the perimeter of the deserted house at least three dozen times until her ankles ached. Again Princesse stayed until the evening to watch the sky over the beach. As she walked along, she picked up a small conch shell and began to blow a song into it.

Princesse wanted to paint the sound that came out of the shell, a moan like a call to a distant ship, an SOS with a dissonant melody. She wanted to paint the feel of the sand beneath her toes, the crackling of dry empty crab shells as she popped them between her palms. She wanted to paint herself, but taller and more curvaceous, with a stream of silky black mermaid's hair. She wanted to discover where the sky and the sea meet each other like two old paramours who had been separated for a very long time.

Princesse carried the conch shell in her hand as she strolled. She dug the sharp tip of the shell into her index finger and drew a few drops of blood. The blood dripped onto the front of her white undershirt, making small blots that sank into the cloth, leaving uneven circles. Princesse sat on the cooling sand on the beach staring at the spots on her otherwise immaculate undershirt, seeing in the blank space all kinds of possibilities.

CATHERINE CAME BACK a week later. Princesse returned to the beach and found her stretched out in a black robe, in her usual lounging chair, reading a magazine.

"Madame," Princesse called from the road, rushing eagerly towards Catherine.

"I am sorry," Catherine said. "I had to go to Paris."

Catherine folded the magazine and started walking back to the house.

As Princesse had expected, all the painted canvases were gone. Catherine offered her some iced rum on the veranda. This time Princesse gladly accepted. She would chew some mint leaves before going home.

Catherine did not notice the bloodstains on the undershirt that Princesse had worn every day since she'd drawn on it with her own blood. Catherine sifted through a portfolio of recent work and pulled out a small painting of Princesse lying naked on the beach rock with a candle in each hand.

"I had a burst of creativity when I was in Paris," she said. "Here, it's yours."

Princesse peered at this re-creation, not immediately recognizing herself, but then seeing in the face, the eyes, the breasts, a very true replication of her body.

Princesse stared at the painting for a long time and then she picked it up, cradling it as though it were a child. It was the first time that Catherine had given *her* one of her paintings. Princesse felt like she had helped to give birth to something that would have never existed otherwise.

"My friend, the artist whose boots I used to wear," Catherine said, "I wanted to go to Paris if only to see his grave. I missed the funeral, but I wanted to see where his bones were resting."

Catherine gave Princesse two T-shirts, one from the Pompidou Center, and another from a museum in Paris where she hoped one day her work would hang.

"I wish I could have let you know I was going," Catherine said. "But I wasn't sure myself that I would go until I got on the plane."

Princesse sat on the veranda next to Catherine, holding her little painting. She was slowly becoming familiar with what she saw there. It was her all right, re-created.

It struck Princesse that this is why she wanted to make pictures, to have something to leave behind even after she was gone, something that showed what she had observed in a way that no one else had and no one else would after her. The sky in all its glory had been there for eons even before she came into the world, and there it would stay with its crashing stars and moody clouds. The sand and its caresses, the conch and its melody would be there forever as well. All that would change would be the faces of the people who would see and touch those things, faces like hers, which was already not as it had been a few years before and which would mature and change in the years to come.

THAT AFTERNOON, as Princesse walked up the road near the cockfights, clutching an image of herself frozen in a time that would never repeat, a man walked out of the yard, carrying a fiery red rooster with a black sock draped over its face. The rooster was still and lifeless beneath the sock even as the man took sips of white rum and blew it in a cloud at the rooster's shrouded head. A few drops of blood fell to the earth in a circle and vanished in the dirt.

Along the fence, the old drunk was moaning a melody that Princesse had never heard him sing before, a sad longing tune that reminded her of the wail of the conch shell.

"I am a lucky man, twice a day I see you," he said.

"Twice a day," she replied.

The old man dug his heel into the dust as his wife approached him, trying to take him home.

Princesse watched the couple from a safe distance, cradling her portrait in her arms. When she was far enough away not to be noticed, she sat on a patch of grass under a tree and began to draw their two faces in the dust. First she drew a silhouette of the old man and then his wife with her basket on her head, perched over him like a ballerina, unaware of her load.

When she was done, Princesse got up and walked away, leaving the blank faces in the dirt for the next curious voyeur to add a stroke to.

In the yard nearby another cockfight had begun.

"Get him, kill him!" the men cheered. "Take his head off. Right now!"

DISCUSSION QUESTIONS

1. "There was nothing so beautiful about her body, Princesse thought. She had a body like all the others who lived here except she was willing to be naked." Consider Princesse's relationship to her body. How does it change over the course of the story?

2. How does Danticat use setting and atmosphere to propel the story?

3. What role does art play in Princesse's self-discovery? What motivates her to pose nude and to pursue these encounters with Catherine?

In a House of Wooden Monkeys

Shay Youngblood

Originally published in 1989

Her clear brown eyes watched, her full dark lips
smiled at her baby, the most happiness she had ever
had in her young life, because she got to keep this one.

Summer rain sounded heavy on the new tin roof. Loud
whispers ran up and down the rough wooden pews.
Father MacIntyre was getting impatient. He knew Moses
would not come and he could not perform the ceremony if Moses
was not there.

"Yate where is Moses? We have waited long enough," the
Father said.

"He soon come Father. He know we waiting for he," the young
woman answered, lowering her eyes to the fat brown baby she
held close to her heart. She didn't seem to notice the impatience
in the air, but her throat was as tight as a witch's drum and her
spine tingled with the tension. On this most important day she
and Moses had fought over the ritual to baptize the baby in Holy
Water to protect it. Moses had raised his hand to slap her, a thing

he had never done, and left before he did. She was in misery, but could not show it before all those who had come to witness.

The child in Yate's arms was restless and cried. Yate carefully opened her worn, white cotton blouse and offered her breast, full with milk, to the child. She guided her tender nipple into her baby's mouth, it sucked noisily. Her clear brown eyes watched, her full dark lips smiled at her baby, the most happiness she had ever had in her young life, because she got to keep this one. She had lost two babies already.

Hill folk said Widow took her babies. The first one Widow drowned in a dream sack, told folk she dreamed Yate's baby would be born dead, and it was. The second time, Widow strangled her baby with the mother's string. Everyone knew Widow had done it. Widow was a toothless young woman who had come to Greenlove Mountain as a girl to live with her grandmother, a rootwoman, in a wood shack by the road. Her grandmother died shortly after she came and as she was strange and thought to be blessed of evil, no one would take her in. So she lived high up on the mountain. She got the name Widow by the birthmark shaped like a black widow spider she carried on her forehead and by her dark attitude and visions of death.

The third time Yate discovered that there was a child growing inside of her, she began to go to Greenlove Mountain church on sundays. The whiteman had come from England to teach her people about his god, who he said was the All Mighty and All Powerful one. He certainly was a rich god. He allowed the priest to dress in fancy velvet robes and white satin hats, to perform grand rituals with white candles set in heavy brass and drink French red wine, he called blood, from an inlaid golden chalice.

Yate burned offerings at the breaking of each day and went to the church services every sunday morning to pray to the white-man's god, hoping his prayer and juju would be stronger than Widow's magic, this time. She prayed with a desperate passion to Jesus and she prayed to the Virgin Mary, whom she pitied, to save her baby. Baby Gillian was born in her Mama Etta's house, arriving lungs filled with fear and clenched fists beating the air that smelled so of blood. Yate cried, praised the Lord and her personal juju. She kissed the Holy Medal she wore around her neck. Moses, he laughed at her, shaking his dreadlocks from side to side at his woman's foolishness.

"It is Jah taking care of thee woman, you betta forget dis jesus nonsense," he said, lighting a bowl of herb, smoke and scent of it rising in the air between them. More had come between them because of her promise to the whiteman's god.

Moses was pleased at the birth of a living child. For two years they had only stolen hours. Mama Etta had kept a sharp eye on her daughter, sending her to town school hoping to keep the young lovers apart. With the birth of Baby Gillian even Mama Etta could not hold Yate, they could live together as man and wife. Mama Etta poured rum into the earth and slit the throat of a baby goat.

For as long as Yate could remember there were babies in Mama Etta's house. Soft, fat, warm, brown babies that cried when pinched, and laughed when teased in tender spots. Mama Etta was a rich woman, because she would always have some-one to care for her. She had fifteen children to her credit. Her sons would provide for her and carry the family name to another generation and her daughters when educated would marry well and visit her often with many grandchildren to warm her lap. To Yate these things were important, to have someone to love you always, a man could leave you. To deliver a living, growing thing from her body was a miracle she wanted to bear. She knew that Mama Etta could not keep her from her man, even though he was a Rastaman, if she were to bear his child. She loved Moses enough, she could feel it in her heart and blood and limbs whenever he watched her undress at the river or touched her body with a reverence and ritual she marveled at when they made love on mossy patches of damp earth beneath the coolness of the waterfall.

Yate promised Jesus she would go up the hill to the whiteman's church every day if her baby was allowed to be among the living, and so she did. When Baby Gillian was born alive and kicking, Yate invited all her friends and family, many of whom had never been to church, to come see her baby be blessed with Holy Water. Some came only for the spectacle, as they were suspicious of a man with only one god.

Saint Julien came because she was Yate's best girlfriend. They were friends and lovers long before she met Moses. Saint Julien's husband was at sea for many months of the year, it was only natural that she longed for hands and lips of passion on her breasts and on the soft spot between her thighs and warm arms to hold her through the endless nights her husband was away. So many men of the village loved the sea. She also could not have a baby by Yate to anger her husband. She often wished that many things were not as they were, but when the men returned from the sea, the women turned from each other in that intimate way, back to their men. It had always been the way, from her grandmother's time and before.

The faithful of the congregation were waiting, hands pressed in respect for the ritual. This was to be the first christening in the church. Four families were present with new babies to be sprinkled with the priest's Holy Water. Father MacIntyre blew his nose into a white lace handkerchief and cleared his throat, as he did when he was about to speak on some important subject in his sunday morning talks to them.

"I can wait no longer. Let us begin," the Father said.

"But my Gillian, will you bless her?" Yate whispered, tears reaching for the edge of her eyes.

The Father turned away from her tears and to those who had come for the ceremony. He was so cold his words chilled like ice.

"A man who would allow his child to be punished for his sins is not a man. If a woman is loose and without moral responsibility, she is the devil's sin and so is her child. In good conscience I cannot perform the rites for Yate's bastard child."

Angry looks flew above the injustice of his words. Up to this point there had been silence, but Mama Etta spilled herself into the room and stepped like a queen up to the altar, to her daughter's side.

"She is a daughter of the gods and loved not less. She ain't belonging to no Rastaman, to no devil, no other woman, just me. I give her life and breath from between these thighs, something you can never do, because it is you who are evil and cannot bear a miracle. You are a no-feeling wooden monkey and so are the people of this house." She spit in the dust before him.

Taking her daughter's arm, they made their way down the aisle and through the doors of the church. Father MacIntyre stood stiffly before the podium and watched helplessly as the pews emptied behind Mama Etta, Yate and Baby Gillian. The silent procession of those who had lost faith wound down the dirt path to the village.

Widow stood grinning in the doorway after most all had gone but the Father. She said a few words that made no sense to human ears, shook some feathers, then squat to pee on the threshold. The remaining of the congregation watched in surprise as the Father seized his throat and choked himself to the ground, where he wallowed like a dog. Widow watched him some, then turned to follow the others.

DISCUSSION QUESTIONS

1. Youngblood writes, "Her clear brown eyes watched, her full dark lips smiled at her baby, the most happiness she had ever had in her young life, because she got to keep this one. She had lost two babies already." What does motherhood mean to Yate? How is she similar to or different from her own mother?

2. Religion and ritual permeate this story. How would you describe Yate's faith? How does it change over the course of the story?

3. How do you interpret the title of the story?

Reena

Paule Marshall

Originally published in 1962

Her real name had been Doreen, a standard for girls
among West Indians (her mother, like my parents,
was from Barbados), but she had changed it to Reena
on her twelfth birthday.

L ike most people with unpleasant childhoods, I am on
constant guard against the past—the past being for
me the people and places associated with the years I
served out my girlhood in Brooklyn. The places no longer matter that much since most of them have vanished. The old gram-
mar school, for instance, P.S. 35 ("Dirty 5's" we called it and
with justification) has been replaced by a low, coldly functional
arrangement of glass and PermaStone which bears its name but
has none of the feel of a school about it. The small, grudgingly
lighted stores along Fulton Street, the soda parlor that was like a
church with its stained-glass panels in the door and marble floor
have given way to those impersonal emporiums, the supermar-
kets. Our house even, a brownstone relic whose halls smelled

comfortingly of dust and lemon oil, the somnolent street upon
which it stood, the tall, muscular trees which shaded it were lev-
eled years ago to make way for a city housing project—a stark,
graceless warren for the poor. So that now whenever I revisit
that old section of Brooklyn and see these new and ugly forms, I
feel nothing. I might as well be in a strange city.

But it is another matter with the people of my past, the faces
that in their darkness were myriad reflections of mine. Whenever I encounter them at the funeral or wake, the wedding or
christening—those ceremonies by which the past reaffirms its
hold—my guard drops and memories banished to the rear of
the mind rush forward to rout the present. I almost become the
child again—anxious and angry, disgracefully diffident.

Reena was one of the people from that time, and a main con-
tributor to my sense of ineffectualness then. She had not done
this deliberately. It was just that whenever she talked about herself (and this was not as often as most people) she seemed to be
talking about me also. She ruthlessly analyzed herself, spar-
ing herself nothing. Her honesty was so absolute it was a kind
of cruelty.

She had not changed, I was to discover in meeting her again
after a separation of twenty years. Nor had I really. For although
the years had altered our positions (she was no longer the lord
and I the lackey) and I could even afford to forgive her now, she
still had the ability to disturb me profoundly by dredging to the
surface those aspects of myself that I kept buried. This time, as
I listened to her talk over the stretch of one long night, she made
vivid without knowing it what is perhaps the most critical fact
of my existence—that definition of me, of her and millions like
us, formulated by others to serve out their fantasies, a definition

we have to combat at an unconscionable cost to the self and even use, at times, in order to survive; the cause of so much shame and rage as well as, oddly enough, a source of pride: simply, what it has meant, what it means, to be a black woman in America.

We met—Reena and myself—at the funeral of her aunt who had been my godmother and whom I had also called aunt, Aunt Vi, and loved, for she and her house had been, respectively, a source of understanding and a place of calm for me as a child. Reena entered the church where the funeral service was being held as though she, not the minister, were coming to officiate, sat down among the immediate family up front, and turned to inspect those behind her. I saw her face then.

It was a good copy of the original. The familiar mold was there, that is, and the configuration of bone beneath the skin was the same despite the slight fleshiness I had never seen there before; her features had even retained their distinctive touches: the positive set to her mouth, the assertive lift to her nose, the same insistent, unsettling eyes which when she was angry became as black as her skin—and this was total, unnerving, and very beautiful. Yet something had happened to her face. It was different despite its sameness. Aging even while it remained enviably young. Time had sketched in, very lightly, the evidence of the twenty years.

As soon as the funeral service was over, I left, hurrying out of the church into the early November night. The wind, already at its winter strength, brought with it the smell of dead leaves and the image of Aunt Vi there in the church, as dead as the leaves—as well as the thought of Reena, whom I would see later at the wake.

Her real name had been Doreen, a standard for girls among

West Indians (her mother, like my parents, was from Barbados), but she had changed it to Reena on her twelfth birthday—"As a present to myself"—and had enforced the change on her family by refusing to answer to the old name. "Reena. With two e's!" she would say and imprint those e's on your mind with the indelible black of her eyes and a thin threatening finger that was like a quill.

She and I had not been friends through our own choice. Rather, our mothers, who had known each other since childhood, had forced the relationship. And from the beginning, I had been at a disadvantage. For Reena, as early as the age of twelve, had had a quality that was unique, superior, and therefore dangerous. She seemed defined, even then, all of a piece, the raw edges of her adolescence smoothed over; indeed, she seemed to have escaped adolescence altogether and made one dazzling leap from childhood into the very arena of adult life. At thirteen, for instance, she was reading Zola, Hauptmann, Steinbeck, while I was still in the thrall of the Little Minister and Lorna Doone. When I could only barely conceive of the world beyond Brooklyn, she was talking of the Civil War in Spain, lynchings in the South, Hitler in Poland—and talking with the outrage and passion of a revolutionary. I would try, I remember, to console myself with the thought that she was really an adult masquerading as a child, which meant that I could not possibly be her match.

For her part, Reena put up with me and was, by turns, patronizing and impatient. I merely served as the audience before whom she rehearsed her ideas and the yardstick by which she measured her worldliness and knowledge.

"Do you realize that this stupid country supplied Japan with the scrap iron to make the weapons she's now using against it?" she had shouted at me once.

I had not known that.

Just as she overwhelmed me, she overwhelmed her family, with the result that despite a half dozen brothers and sisters who consumed quantities of bread and jam whenever they visited us, she behaved like an only child and got away with it. Her father, a gentle man with skin the color of dried tobacco and with the nose Reena had inherited jutting out like a crag from his nondescript face, had come from Georgia and was always making jokes about having married a foreigner—Reena's mother being from the West Indies. When not joking, he seemed slightly bewildered by his large family and so in awe of Reena that he avoided her. Reena's mother, a small, dry, formidably black woman, was less a person to me than the abstract principle of force, power, energy. She was alternately strict and indulgent with Reena and, despite the inconsistency, surprisingly effective.

They lived when I knew them in a cold-water railroad flat above a kosher butcher on Belmont Avenue in Brownsville, some distance from us—and this in itself added to Reena's exotic quality. For it was a place where Sunday became Saturday, with all the stores open and pushcarts piled with vegetables and yard goods lined up along the curb, a crowded place where people hawked and spat freely in the streaming gutters and the men looked as if they had just stepped from the pages of the Old Testament with their profuse beards and long, black, satin coats.

When Reena was fifteen her family moved to Jamaica in Queens and since, in those days, Jamaica was considered too far away for visiting, our families lost contact and I did not see

Reena again until we were both in college and then only once and not to speak to. . . .

I had walked some distance and by the time I got to the wake, which was being held at Aunt Vi's house, it was well under way. It was a good wake. Aunt Vi would have been pleased. There was plenty to drink, and more than enough to eat, including some Barbadian favorites: coconut bread, pone made with the cassava root, and the little crisp codfish cakes that are so hot with peppers they bring tears to the eyes as you bite into them.

I had missed the beginning, when everyone had probably sat around talking about Aunt Vi and recalling the few events that had distinguished her otherwise undistinguished life. (Someone, I'm sure, had told of the time she had missed the excursion boat to Atlantic City and had her own private picnic—complete with pigeon peas and rice and fricassee chicken—on the pier at 42nd Street.) By the time I arrived, though, it would have been indiscreet to mention her name, for by then the wake had become— and this would also have pleased her—a celebration of life.

I had had two drinks, one right after the other, and was well into my third when Reena, who must have been upstairs, entered the basement kitchen where I was. She saw me before I had quite seen her, and with a cry that alerted the entire room to her presence and charged the air with her special force, she rushed toward me.

"Hey, I'm the one who was supposed to be the writer, not you! Do you know, I still can't believe it," she said, stepping back, her blackness heightened by a white mocking smile. "I read both your books over and over again and I can't really believe it. My Little Paulie!"

I did not mind. For there was respect and even wonder

behind the patronizing words and in her eyes. The old imbal-
ance between us had ended and I was suddenly glad to see her.

I told her so and we both began talking at once, but Reena's
voice overpowered mine, so that all I could do after a time was
listen while she discussed my books, and dutifully answer her
questions about my personal life.

"And what about you?" I said, almost brutally, at the first
chance I got. "What've you been up to all this time?"

She got up abruptly. "Good Lord, in here's noisy as hell. Come
on, let's go upstairs."

We got fresh drinks and went up to Aunt Vi's bedroom, where
in the soft light from the lamps, the huge Victorian bed and the
pink satin bedspread with roses of the same material strewn
over its surface looked as if they had never been used. And, in
a way, this was true. Aunt Vi had seldom slept in her bed or, for
that matter, lived in her house, because in order to pay for it, she
had had to work at a sleeping-in job which gave her only Thursdays and every other Sunday off.

Reena sat on the bed, crushing the roses, and I sat on one of
the numerous trunks which crowded the room. They contained
every dress, coat, hat, and shoe that Aunt Vi had worn since
coming to the United States. I again asked Reena what she had
been doing over the years.

"Do you want a blow-by-blow account?" she said. But despite
the flippancy, she was suddenly serious. And when she began
it was clear that she had written out the narrative in her mind
many times. The words came too easily; the events, the incidents
had been ordered in time, and the meaning of her behavior and
of the people with whom she had been involved had been pains-
takingly analyzed. She talked willingly, with desperation almost.

And the words by themselves weren't enough. She used her hands to give them form and urgency. I became totally involved with her and all that she said. So much so that as the night wore on I was not certain at times whether it was she or I speaking.

From the time her family moved to Jamaica until she was nineteen or so, Reena's life sounded, from what she told me in the beginning, as ordinary as mine and most of the girls we knew. After high school she had gone on to one of the free city colleges, where she had majored in journalism, worked part time in the school library, and, surprisingly enough, joined a houseplan. (Even I hadn't gone that far.) It was an all-Negro club, since there was a tacit understanding that Negro and white girls did not join each other's houseplans. "Integration, Northern style," she said, shrugging.

It seems that Reena had had a purpose and a plan in joining the group. "I thought," she said with a wry smile, "I could get those girls up off their complacent rumps and out doing something about social issues. . . . I couldn't get them to budge. I remember after the war when a Negro ex-soldier had his eyes gouged out by a bus driver down South I tried getting them to demonstrate on campus. I talked until I was hoarse, but to no avail. They were too busy planning the annual autumn frolic."

Her laugh was bitter but forgiving and it ended in a long, reflective silence. After which she said quietly, "It wasn't that they didn't give a damn. It was just, I suppose, that like most people they didn't want to get involved to the extent that they might have to stand up and be counted. If it ever came to that. Then another thing. They thought they were safe, special. After all, they had grown up in the North, most of them, and so had escaped the southern-style prejudice; their parents, like mine, were struggling to put them through college; they could look forward to being tidy little schoolteachers, social workers, and lab technicians. Oh, they were safe!" The sarcasm scored her voice and then abruptly gave way to pity. "Poor things, they weren't safe, you see, and would never be as long as millions like themselves in Harlem, on Chicago's South Side, down South, all over the place, were unsafe. I tried to tell them this—and they accused me of being oversensitive. They tried not to listen. But I would have held out and, I'm sure, even brought some of them around eventually if this other business with a silly boy hadn't happened at the same time. . . ."

Reena told me then about her first, brief, and apparently innocent affair with a boy she had met at one of the houseplan parties. It had ended, she said, when the boy's parents had met her. "That was it," she said and the flat of her hand cut into the air. "He was forbidden to see me. The reason? He couldn't bring himself to tell me, but I knew. I was too black.

"Naturally, it wasn't the first time something like that had happened. In fact, you might say that was the theme of my childhood. Because I was dark I was always being plastered with Vaseline so I wouldn't look ashy. Whenever I had my picture taken they would pile a whitish powder on my face and make the lights so bright I always came out looking ghostly. My mother stopped speaking to any number of people because they said I would have been pretty if I hadn't been so dark. Like nearly every little black girl, I had my share of dreams of waking up to find myself with long, blond curls, blue eyes, and skin like milk. So I should have been prepared. Besides, that boy's parents were really rejecting themselves in rejecting me.

"Take us"—and her hands, opening in front of my face as she

suddenly leaned forward, seemed to offer me the whole of black humanity. "We live surrounded by white images, and white in this world is synonymous with the good, light, beauty, success, so that, despite ourselves sometimes, we run after that whiteness and deny our darkness, which has been made into the symbol of all that is evil and inferior. I wasn't a person to that boy's parents, but a symbol of the darkness they were in flight from, so that just as they—that boy, his parents, those silly girls in the houseplan— were running from me, I started running from them. . . ."

It must have been shortly after this happened when I saw Reena at a debate which was being held at my college. She did not see me, since she was one of the speakers and I was merely part of her audience in the crowded auditorium. The topic had some- thing to do with intellectual freedom in the colleges (McCar- thyism was coming into vogue then) and aside from a Jewish boy from City College, Reena was the most effective—sharp, pro- vocative, her position the most radical. The others on the panel seemed intimidated not only by the strength and cogency of her argument but by the sheer impact of her blackness in their white midst.

Her color might have been a weapon she used to dazzle and disarm her opponents. And she had highlighted it with the clothes she was wearing: a white dress patterned with large blocks of primary colors I remember (it looked Mexican) and a pair of intricately wrought silver earrings—long and with many little parts which clashed like muted cymbals over the micro- phone each time she moved her head. She wore her hair cropped short like a boy's and it was not straightened like mine and the other Negro girls' in the audience, but left in its coarse natural state: a small forest under which her face emerged in its intense and startling handsomeness. I remember she left the auditorium in triumph that day, surrounded by a noisy entourage from her college—all of them white.

"We were very serious," she said now, describing the left-wing group she had belonged to then—and there was a defensiveness in her voice which sought to protect them from all censure. "We believed—because we were young, I suppose, and had nothing as yet to risk—that we could do something about the injustices which everyone around us seemed to take for granted. So we picketed and demonstrated and bombarded Washington with our protests, only to have our names added to the Attorney General's list for all our trouble. We were always standing on street corners handing out leaflets or getting people to sign petitions. We always seemed to pick the coldest days to do that." Her smile held long after the words had died.

"I, we all, had such a sense of purpose then," she said softly, and a sadness lay aslant the smile now, darkening it. "We were forever holding meetings, having endless discussions, arguing, shouting, theorizing. And we had fun. Those parties! There was always somebody with a guitar. We were always singing. . . ." Suddenly, she began singing—and her voice was sure, militant, and faintly self-mocking,

> *"But the banks are made of marble*
>   *With a guard at every door*
> *And the vaults are stuffed with silver*
>   *That the workers sweated for . . ."*

When she spoke again the words were a sad coda to the song. "Well, as you probably know, things came to an ugly head with

McCarthy reigning in Washington, and I was one of the people temporarily suspended from school."

She broke off and we both waited, the ice in our glasses melted and the drinks gone flat.

"At first, I didn't mind," she said finally. "After all, we were right. The fact that they suspended us proved it. Besides, I was in the middle of an affair, a real one this time, and too busy with that to care about anything else." She paused again, frowning.

"He was white," she said quickly and glanced at me as though to surprise either shock or disapproval in my face. "We were very involved. At one point—I think just after we had been suspended and he started working—we even thought of getting married. Living in New York, moving in the crowd we did, we might have been able to manage it. But I couldn't. There were too many complex things going on beneath the surface," she said, her voice strained by the hopelessness she must have felt then, her hands shaping it in the air between us. "Neither one of us could really escape what our color had come to mean in this country. Let me explain. Bob was always, for some odd reason, talking about how much the Negro suffered, and although I would agree with him I would also try to get across that, you know, like all people we also had fun once in a while, loved our children, liked making love—that we were human beings, for God's sake. But he only wanted to hear about the suffering. It was as if this comforted him and eased his own suffering—and he did suffer because of any number of things: his own uncertainty, for one, his difficulties with his family, for another . . .

"Once, I remember, when his father came into New York, Bob insisted that I meet him. I don't know why I agreed to go with him. . . ." She took a deep breath and raised her head very high. "I'll never forget or forgive the look on that old man's face when he opened his hotel-room door and saw me. The horror. I might have been the personification of every evil in the world. His inability to believe that it was his son standing there holding my hand. His shock. I'm sure he never fully recovered. I know I never did. Nor can I forget Bob's laugh in the elevator afterwards, the way he kept repeating: 'Did you see his face when he saw you? Did you? . . .' He had used me, you see. I had been the means, the instrument of his revenge.

"And I wasn't any better. I used him. I took every opportunity to treat him shabbily, trying, you see, through him, to get at that white world which had not only denied me, but had turned my own against me." Her eyes closed. "I went numb all over when I understood what we were doing to, and with, each other. I stayed numb for a long time."

As Reena described the events which followed—the break with Bob, her gradual withdrawal from the left-wing group ("I had had it with them too. I got tired of being 'their Negro,' their pet. Besides, they were just all talk, really. All theories and abstractions. I doubt that, with all their elaborate plans for the Negro and for the workers of the world, any of them had ever been near a factory or up to Harlem")—as she spoke about her reinstatement in school, her voice suggested the numbness she had felt then. It only stirred into life again when she talked of her graduation.

"You should have seen my parents. It was really their day. My mother was so proud she complained about everything: her seat, the heat, the speaker; and my father just sat there long after everybody had left, too awed to move. God, it meant so much to them. It was as if I had made up for the generations his people had picked cotton in Georgia and my mother's family had cut cane in the West Indies. It frightened me."

I asked her after a long wait what she had done after graduating.

"How do you mean, what I did. Looked for a job. Tell me, have you ever looked for work in this man's city?"

"I know," I said, holding up my hand. "Don't tell me."

We both looked at my raised hand which sought to waive the discussion, then at each other and suddenly we laughed, a laugh so loud and violent with pain and outrage it brought tears.

"Girl," Reena said, the tears silver against her blackness. "You could put me blindfolded right now at the Times Building on 42nd Street and I would be able to find my way to every newspaper office in town. But tell me, how come white folks is so *hard*?"

"Just bo'n hard."

We were laughing again and this time I nearly slid off the trunk and Reena fell back among the satin roses.

"I didn't know there were so many ways of saying 'no' without ever once using the word," she said, the laughter lodged in her throat, but her eyes had gone hard. "Sometimes I'd find myself in the elevator, on my way out, and smiling all over myself because I thought I had gotten the job, before it would hit me that they had really said no, not yes. Some of those people in personnel had so perfected their smiles they looked almost genuine. The ones who used to get me, though, were those who tried to make the interview into an intimate chat between friends. They'd put you in a comfortable chair, offer you a cigarette, and order coffee. How I hated that coffee. They didn't know it—or maybe they did—but it was like offering me hemlock. . . .

"You think Christ had it tough?" Her laughter rushed against the air which resisted it. "I was crucified five days a week and half-day on Saturday. I became almost paranoid. I began to think there might be something other than color wrong with me which everybody but me could see, some rare disease that had turned me into a monster.

"My parents suffered. And that bothered me most, because I felt I had failed them. My father didn't say anything but I knew because he avoided me more than usual. He was ashamed, I think, that he hadn't been able, as a man and as my father, to prevent this. My mother—well, you know her. In one breath she would try to comfort me by cursing them: 'But Gor blind them'"—and Reena's voice captured her mother's aggressive accent—"'if you had come looking for a job mopping down their floors they would o' hire you, the brutes. But mark my words, their time goin' come, cause God don't love ugly and he ain't stuck on pretty . . .' And in the next breath she would curse me, 'Journalism! Journalism! Whoever heard of colored people taking up journalism. You must feel you's white or something so. The people is right to chuck you out their office. . . .' Poor thing, to make up for saying all that she would wash my white gloves every night and cook cereal for me in the morning as if I were a little girl again. Once she went out and bought me a suit she couldn't afford from Lord and Taylor's. I looked like a Smith girl in blackface in it. . . . So guess where I ended up?"

"As a social investigator for the Welfare Department. Where else?"

We were helpless with laughter again.

"You too?"

"No," I said, "I taught, but that was just as bad."

"No," she said, sobering abruptly. "Nothing's as bad as working for Welfare. Do you know what they really mean by a social investigator? A spy. Someone whose dirty job it is to snoop into the corners of the lives of the poor and make their poverty more vivid by taking from them the last shred of privacy. 'Mrs. Jones, is that a new dress you're wearing?' 'Mrs. Brown, this kerosene heater is not listed in the household items. Did you get an authorization for it?' 'Mrs. Smith, is that a telephone I hear ringing under the sofa?' I was utterly demoralized within a month.

"And another thing. I thought I knew about poverty. I mean, I remember, as a child, having to eat soup made with those white beans the government used to give out free for days running, sometimes, because there was nothing else. I had lived in Brownsville, among all the poor Jews and Poles and Irish there. But what I saw in Harlem, where I had my case load, was different somehow. Perhaps because it seemed so final. There didn't seem to be any way to escape from those dark hallways and dingy furnished rooms. . . . All that defeat." Closing her eyes, she finished the stale whiskey and soda in her glass.

"I remember a client of mine, a girl my age with three children already and no father for them and living in the expensive squalor of a rooming house. Her bewilderment. Her resignation. Her anger. She could have pulled herself out of the mess she was in? People say that, you know, including some Negroes. But this girl didn't have a chance. She had been trapped from the day she was born in some small town down South.

"She became my reference. From then on and even now, whenever I hear people and groups coming up with all kinds of solutions to the quote Negro problem, I ask one question. What

are they really doing for that girl, to save her or to save the children? . . . The answer isn't very encouraging."

It was some time before she continued, and then she told me
that after Welfare she had gone to work for a private social-work
agency, in their publicity department, and had started on her
master's in journalism at Columbia. She also left home around
this time.

"I had to. My mother started putting the pressure on me to
get married. The hints, the remarks—and you know my mother
was never the subtle type—her anxiety, which made me anxious
about getting married after a while. Besides, it was time for me
to be on my own."

In contrast to the unmistakably radical character of her late
adolescence (her membership in the left-wing group, the affair
with Bob, her suspension from college), Reena's life of this period
sounded ordinary, standard—and she admitted it with a slightly
self-deprecating, apologetic smile. It was similar to that of any
number of unmarried professional Negro women in New York
or Los Angeles or Washington: the job teaching or doing social
work which brought in a fairly decent salary, the small apartment with kitchenette which they sometimes shared with a
roommate; a car, some of them; membership in various political
and social action organizations for the militant few like Reena;
the vacations in Mexico, Europe, the West Indies, and now
Africa; the occasional date. "The interesting men were invari-
ably married," Reena said and then mentioned having had one
affair during that time. She had found out he was married and
had thought of her only as the perfect mistress. "The bastard,"
she said, but her smile forgave him.

"Women alone!" she cried, laughing sadly, and her raised

opened arms, the empty glass she held in one hand made eloquent their aloneness. "Alone and lonely, and indulging themselves while they wait. The girls of the houseplan have reached
their majority only to find that all those years they spent accu-
mulating their degrees and finding the well-paying jobs in the
hope that this would raise their stock have, instead, put them
at a disadvantage. For the few eligible men around—those who
are their intellectual and professional peers, whom they can
respect (and there are very few of them)—don't necessarily
marry them, but younger women without the degrees and the
fat jobs, who are no threat, or they don't marry at all because
they are either queer or mother-ridden. Or they marry white
women. Now, intellectually I accept this. In fact, some of my
best friends are white women..." And again our laughter—
that loud, searing burst which we used to cauterize our hurt
mounted into the unaccepting silence of the room. "After all,
our goal is a fully integrated society. And perhaps, as some people believe, the only solution to the race problem is miscege-
nation. Besides, a man should be able to marry whomever he
wishes. Emotionally, though, I am less kind and understanding,
and I resent like hell the reasons some black men give for rejecting us for them."

"We're too middle-class-oriented," I said. "Conservative."

"Right. Even though, thank God, that doesn't apply to me."

"Too threatening... castrating..."

"Too independent and impatient with them for not being
more ambitious... contemptuous..."

"Sexually inhibited and unimaginative..."

"And the old myth of the excessive sexuality of the black
woman goes out the window," Reena cried.

"Not supportive, unwilling to submerge our interests for theirs . . ."

"Lacking in the subtle art of getting and keeping a man . . ."

We had recited the accusations in the form and tone of a litany, and in the silence which followed we shared a thin, hopeless smile.

"They condemn us," Reena said softly but with anger, "without taking history into account. We are still, most of us, the black woman who had to be almost frighteningly strong in order for us all to survive. For, after all, she was the one whom they left (and I don't hold this against them; I understand) with the children to raise, who had to *make* it somehow or the other. And we are still, so many of us, living that history.

"You would think that they would understand this, but few do. So it's up to us. We have got to understand them and save them for ourselves. How? By being, on one hand, persons in our own right and, on the other, fully the woman and the wife. . . . Christ, listen to who's talking! I had my chance. And I tried. Very hard. But it wasn't enough."

The festive sounds of the wake had died to a sober murmur beyond the bedroom. The crowd had gone, leaving only Reena and myself upstairs and the last of Aunt Vi's closest friends in the basement below. They were drinking coffee. I smelled it, felt its warmth and intimacy in the empty house, heard the distant tapping of the cups against the saucers and voices muted by grief. The wake had come full circle: they were again mourning Aunt Vi.

And Reena might have been mourning with them, sitting there amid the satin roses, framed by the massive headboard. Her hands lay as if they had been broken in her lap. Her eyes were like those of someone blind or dead. I got up to go and get some coffee for her.

"You met my husband," she said quickly, stopping me.

"Have I?" I said, sitting down again.

"Yes, before we were married even. At an autograph party for you. He was freelancing—he's a photographer—and one of the Negro magazines had sent him to cover the party."

As she went on to describe him I remembered him vaguely, not his face, but his rather large body stretching and bending with a dancer's fluidity and grace as he took the pictures. I had heard him talking to a group of people about some issue on race relations very much in the news then and had been struck by his vehemence. For the moment I had found this almost odd, since he was so fair skinned he could have passed for white.

They had met, Reena told me now, at a benefit show for a Harlem day nursery given by one of the progressive groups she belonged to, and had married a month afterward. From all that she said they had had a full and exciting life for a long time. Her words were so vivid that I could almost see them: she with her startling blackness and extraordinary force and he with his near-white skin and a militancy which matched hers; both of them moving among the disaffected in New York, their stand on political and social issues equally uncompromising, the line of their allegiance reaching directly to all those trapped in Harlem. And they had lived the meaning of this allegiance, so that even when they could have afforded a life among the black bourgeoisie of St. Albans or Teaneck, they had chosen to live if not in Harlem so close that there was no difference.

"I—we—were so happy I was frightened at times. Not that anything would change between us, but that someone or something in the world outside us would invade our private place and destroy us out of envy. Perhaps this is what did happen. . . ." She shrugged and even tried to smile but she could not manage it. "Something slipped in while we weren't looking and began its deadly work.

"Maybe it started when Dave took a job with a Negro magazine. I'm not sure. Anyway, in no time, he hated it: the routine, unimaginative pictures he had to take and the magazine itself, which dealt only in unrealities: the high-society world of the black bourgeoisie and the spectacular strides Negroes were making in all fields—you know the type. Yet Dave wouldn't leave. It wasn't the money, but a kind of safety which he had never experienced before which kept him there. He would talk about freelancing again, about storming the gates of the white magazines downtown, of opening his own studio but he never acted on any one of these things. You see, despite his talent—and he was very talented—he had a diffidence that was fatal.

"When I understood this I literally forced him to open the studio—and perhaps I should have been more subtle and indirect, but that's not my nature. Besides, I was frightened and desperate to help. Nothing happened for a time. Dave's work was too experimental to be commercial. Gradually, though, his photographs started appearing in the prestige camera magazines and money from various awards and exhibits and an occasional assignment started coming in.

"This wasn't enough somehow. Dave also wanted the big, gaudy commercial success that would dazzle and confound that white world downtown and force it to *see* him. And yet, as I said before, he couldn't bring himself to try—and this contradiction began to get to him after a while.

"It was then, I think, that I began to fail him. I didn't know how to help, you see. I had never felt so inadequate before. And this was very strange and disturbing for someone like me. I was being submerged in his problems—and I began fighting against this.

"I started working again (I had stopped after the second baby). And I was lucky because I got back my old job. And unlucky because Dave saw it as my way of pointing up his deficiencies. I couldn't convince him otherwise: that I had to do it for my own sanity. He would accuse me of wanting to see him fail, of trapping him in all kinds of responsibilities. . . . After a time we both got caught up in this thing, an ugliness came between us, and I began to answer his anger with anger and to trade him insult for insult.

"Things fell apart very quickly after that. I couldn't bear the pain of living with him—the insults, our mutual despair, his mocking, the silence. I couldn't subject the children to it any longer. The divorce didn't take long. And thank God, because of the children, we are pleasant when we have to see each other. He's making out very well, I hear."

She said nothing more, but simply bowed her head as though waiting for me to pass judgment on her. I don't know how long we remained like this; but when Reena finally raised her head, the darkness at the window had vanished and dawn was a still, gray smoke against the pane.

"Do you know," she said, and her eyes were clear and a smile had won out over pain, "I enjoy being alone. I don't tell people this because they'll accuse me of either lying or deluding myself. But I do. Perhaps, as my mother tells me, it's only temporary. I don't think so, though. I feel I don't ever want to be involved again. It's not that I've lost interest in men. I go out occasionally, but it's never anything serious. You see, I have all that I want for now."

Her children first of all, she told me, and from her description they sounded intelligent and capable. She was a friend as well as a mother to them, it seemed. They were planning, the four of them, to spend the summer touring Canada. "I will feel that I have done well by them if I give them, if nothing more, a sense of themselves and their worth and importance as black people. Everything I do with them, for them, is to this end. I don't want them ever to be confused about this. They must have their identifications straight from the beginning. No white dolls for them!"

Then her job. She was working now as a researcher for a small progressive news magazine with the promise that once she completed her master's in journalism (she was working on the thesis now) she might get a chance to do some minor reporting. And like most people, she hoped to write someday. "If I can ever stop talking away my substance," she said laughing.

And she was still active in any number of social action groups. In another week or so she would be heading a delegation of mothers down to City Hall "to give the mayor a little hell about conditions in the schools in Harlem." She had started an organization that was carrying on an almost door-to-door campaign in her neighborhood to expose, as she put it, "the bloodsuckers: all those slumlords and storekeepers with their fixed scales, the finance companies that never tell you the real price of a thing, the petty salesmen that leech off the poor...." In May she was taking her two older girls on a nationwide pilgrimage to Washington to urge for a more rapid implementation of the school desegregation law.

"It's uncanny," she said, and the laugh which accompanied the words was warm, soft with wonder at herself, girlish even, and the air in the room which had refused her laughter before rushed to absorb this now. "Really uncanny. Here I am, practically middle-aged, with three children to raise by myself and with little or no money to do it, and yet I feel, strangely enough, as though life is just beginning—that it's new and fresh with all kinds of possibilities. Maybe it's because I've been through my purgatory and I can't ever be overwhelmed again. I don't know. Anyway, you should see me on evenings after I put the children to bed. I sit alone in the living room (I've repainted it and changed all the furniture since Dave's gone, so that it would at least look different)—I sit there making plans and all of them seem possible. The most important plan right now is Africa. I've already started saving the fare."

I asked her whether she was planning to live there permanently and she said simply, "I want to live and work there. For how long, for a lifetime, I can't say. All I know is that I have to. For myself and for my children. It is important that they see black people who have truly a place and history of their own and who are building for a new and, hopefully, more sensible world. And I must see it, get close to it, because I can never lose the sense of being a displaced person here in America because of my color. Oh, I know I should remain and fight not only for integration (even though, frankly, I question whether I want to be integrated into America as it stands now, with its complacency and materialism, its soullessness) but to help change the country into something better, sounder—if that is still possible. But I have to go to Africa. . . .

"Poor Aunt Vi," she said after a long silence and straightened one of the roses she had crushed. "She never really got to enjoy her bed of roses what with only Thursdays and every other Sunday off. All that hard work. All her life. . . . Our lives have got to make more sense, if only for her."

We got up to leave shortly afterward. Reena was staying on to attend the burial, later in the morning, but I was taking the subway to Manhattan. We parted with the usual promise to get together and exchanged telephone numbers. And Reena did phone a week or so later. I don't remember what we talked about though.

Some months later I invited her to a party I was giving before leaving the country. But she did not come.

DISCUSSION QUESTIONS

1. Reena, like Wangero in Alice Walker's "Everyday Use," changes her name. Consider the significance of a name change. How might it have contributed to the personas of these characters?

2. Why do you think Marshall wrote this story in the past tense? How would it read differently if Reena's story were told strictly from her perspective? What do we gain from the narrator?

3. Marshall writes, "In contrast to the unmistakably radical character of her late adolescence . . . Reena's life of this period sounded ordinary, standard—and she admitted it with a slightly self-deprecating, apologetic smile." How does Reena's story make you feel? How do you interpret the bursts of laughter?

Epilogue

How It Feels to Be Colored Me

Zora Neale Hurston

Originally published in 1928

But changes came in the family when I was thirteen, and I was sent to school in Jacksonville. I left Eatonville, the town of the oleanders, a Zora. When I disembarked from the river-boat at Jacksonville, she was no more. It seemed that I had suffered a sea change. I was not Zora of Orange County any more, I was now a little colored girl. I found it out in certain ways. In my heart as well as in the mirror, I became a fast brown— warranted not to rub nor run.

I am colored but I offer nothing in the way of extenuating circumstances except the fact that I am the only Negro in the United States whose grandfather on the mother's side was *not* an Indian chief.

I remember the very day that I became colored. Up to my thirteenth year I lived in the little Negro town of Eatonville, Florida. It is exclusively a colored town. The only white people I knew passed through the town going to or coming from Orlando. The native whites rode dusty horses, the Northern tourists chugged down the sandy village road in automobiles. The town knew the Southerners and never stopped cane chewing when they passed. But the Northerners were something else again. They were peered at cautiously from behind curtains by the timid. The more venturesome would come out on the porch to watch them go past and got just as much pleasure out of the tourists as the tourists got out of the village.

The front porch might seem a daring place for the rest of the town, but it was a gallery seat for me. My favorite place was atop the gatepost. Proscenium box for a born first-nighter. Not only did I enjoy the show, but I didn't mind the actors knowing that I liked it. I usually spoke to them in passing. I'd wave at them and when they returned my salute, I would say something like this: "Howdy-do-well-I-thank-you-where-you-goin'?" Usually automobile or the horse paused at this, and after a queer exchange of compliments, I would probably "go a piece of the way" with them, as we say in farthest Florida. If one of my family happened to come to the front in time to see me, of course negotiations would be rudely broken off. But even so, it is clear that I was the first "welcome-to-our-state" Floridian, and I hope the Miami Chamber of Commerce will please take notice.

During this period, white people differed from colored to me only in that they rode through town and never lived there. They liked to hear me "speak pieces" and sing and wanted to see me dance the parse-me-la, and gave me generously of their small silver for doing these things, which seemed strange to me for I wanted to do them so much that I needed bribing to stop, only they didn't know it. The colored people gave no dimes. They deplored any joyful tendencies in me, but I was their Zora nevertheless. I belonged to them, to the nearby hotels, to the county—everybody's Zora.

But changes came in the family when I was thirteen, and I was sent to school in Jacksonville. I left Eatonville, the town of the oleanders, a Zora. When I disembarked from the river-boat at Jacksonville, she was no more. It seemed that I had suffered a sea change. I was not Zora of Orange County any more, I was now a little colored girl. I found it out in certain ways. In my heart as well as in the mirror, I became a fast brown—warranted not to rub nor run.

But I am not tragically colored. There is no great sorrow dammed up in my soul, nor lurking behind my eyes. I do not mind at all. I do not belong to the sobbing school of Negro-hood who hold that nature somehow has given them a low-down dirty deal and whose feelings are all but about it. Even in the helter-skelter skirmish that is my life, I have seen that the world is to the strong regardless of a little pigmentation more or less. No, I do not weep at the world—I am too busy sharpening my oyster knife.

Someone is always at my elbow reminding me that I am the granddaughter of slaves. It fails to register depression with me. Slavery is sixty years in the past. The operation was successful and the patient is doing well, thank you. The terrible struggle that made me an American out of a potential slave said "On the line!" The Reconstruction said "Get set!" and the generation before said "Go!" I am off to a flying start and I must not halt in the stretch to look behind and weep. Slavery is the price I paid for civilization, and the choice was not with me. It is a bully adventure and worth all that I have paid through my ancestors for it. No one on earth ever had a greater chance for glory. The world to be won and nothing to be lost. It is thrilling to think—to know that for any act of mine, I shall get twice as much praise or twice as much blame. It is quite exciting to hold the center of the national stage, with the spectators not knowing whether to laugh or to weep.

The position of my white neighbor is much more difficult. No brown specter pulls up a chair beside me when I sit down to eat. No dark ghost thrusts its leg against mine in bed. The game of keeping what one has is never so exciting as the game of getting.

I do not always feel colored. Even now I often achieve the unconscious Zora of Eatonville before the Hegira. I feel most colored when I am thrown against a sharp white background.

For instance at Barnard. "Beside the waters of the Hudson" I feel my race. Among the thousand white persons, I am a dark rock surged upon, and overswept, but through it all, I remain myself. When covered by the waters, I am; and the ebb but reveals me again.

Sometimes it is the other way around. A white person is set down in our midst, but the contrast is just as sharp for me. For instance, when I sit in the drafty basement that is The New World Cabaret with a white person, my color comes. We enter chatting about any little nothing that we have in common and are seated by the jazz waiters. In the abrupt way that jazz orchestras have, this one plunges into a number. It loses no time in circumlocutions, but gets right down to business. It constricts the thorax and splits the heart with its tempo and narcotic harmonies. This orchestra grows rambunctious, rears on its hind legs and attacks the tonal veil with primitive fury, rending it, clawing it until it breaks through to the jungle beyond. I follow those heathen—follow them exultingly. I dance wildly inside myself; I yell within, I whoop; I shake my assegai above my head, I hurl it true to the mark yeeeeooww! I am in the jungle and living in the jungle way. My face is painted red and yellow and my body is painted blue. My pulse is throbbing like a war drum. I want to slaughter something—give pain, give death to what, I do not know. But the piece ends. The men of the orchestra wipe their lips and rest their fingers. I creep back slowly to the veneer we call civilization with the last tone and find the white friend sitting motionless in his seat, smoking calmly.

"Good music they have here," he remarks, drumming the table with his fingertips.

Music. The great blobs of purple and red emotion have not touched him. He has only heard what I felt. He is far away and I see him but dimly across the ocean and the continent that have fallen between us. He is so pale with his whiteness then and I am so colored.

At certain times I have no race, I am me. When I set my hat at a certain angle and saunter down Seventh Avenue, Harlem City, feeling as snooty as the lions in front of the Forty-Second Street Library, for instance. So far as my feelings are concerned, Peggy Hopkins Joyce on the Boule Mich with her gorgeous raiment, stately carriage, knees knocking together in a most aristocratic manner, has nothing on me. The cosmic Zora emerges. I belong to no race nor time. I am the eternal feminine with its string of beads.

I have no separate feeling about being an American citizen and colored. I am merely a fragment of the Great Soul that surges within the boundaries. My country, right or wrong.

Sometimes, I feel discriminated against, but it does not make

me angry. It merely astonishes me. How can any deny themselves the pleasure of my company? It's beyond me.

But in the main, I feel like a brown bag of miscellany propped
against a wall. Against a wall in company with other bags, white,
red and yellow. Pour out the contents, and there is discovered
a jumble of small things priceless and worthless. A first-water
diamond, an empty spool, bits of broken glass, lengths of string,
a key to a door long since crumbled away, a rusty knife-blade, old
shoes saved for a road that never was and never will be, a nail
bent under the weight of things too heavy for any nail, a dried
flower or two still a little fragrant. In your hand is the brown
bag. On the ground before you is the jumble it held—so much
like the jumble in the bags, could they be emptied, that all might
be dumped in a single heap and the bags refilled without alter-
ing the content of any greatly. A bit of colored glass more or less
would not matter. Perhaps that is how the Great Stuffer of Bags
filled them in the first place—who knows?

Acknowledgments

I offer my heartfelt gratitude to everyone reading this book and striving to protect Black girlhood, especially the incredible members of the Well-Read Black Girl community. I am forever grateful for your love and support.

Thank you to the entire Norton team, especially my wonderful editor, Gina Iaquinta, and Cordelia Calvert, who worked so diligently to make this collection a reality. I am so lucky to work with you two!

To my brilliant agent Emma Parry: The words *thank you* are never enough. I appreciate your wisdom and sharp insight.

Special thanks to Melissa Flamson and Janet Woods, whose unstinting commitment and precise research made this book possible.

To my favorite Well-Read Black Girl coconspirator Maghan Baptiste: your attention to detail, love of poetry, and unconditional support for my work is a blessing.

To the exceptional writers in this collection whose work continually inspires me: Jamaica Kincaid, Toni Morrison, Dorothy West, Rita Dove, Camille Acker, Toni Cade Bambara, Amina

Gautier, Alexia Arthurs, Dana Johnson, Alice Walker, Gwendolyn Brooks, Edwidge Danticat, Shay Youngblood, Paule Marshall, and Zora Neale Hurston. They are part of a storied legacy, each one crafting powerful images of Black girlhood that will forever inspire and affirm future generations.

I am grateful for the ancestors, the foremothers who guide my mission and make my life's work possible.

Lastly, thank you to my beautiful family for their love and unwavering support. To my brightest light, my son, Zikomo. Thank you for choosing me.

Further Reading

Quicksand by Nella Larsen (1928)

Their Eyes Were Watching God by Zora Neale Hurston (1937)

Maud Martha by Gwendolyn Brooks (1953)

Brown Girl, Brownstones by Paule Marshall (1959)

Jubilee by Margaret Walker (1966)

I Know Why the Caged Bird Sings by Maya Angelou (1969)

The Bluest Eye by Toni Morrison (1970)

Daddy Was a Number Runner by Louise Meriwether (1970)

The Friends by Rosa Guy (1973)

Roll of Thunder, Hear My Cry by Mildred D. Taylor (1976)

Sassafrass, Cypress, and Indigo by Ntozake Shange (1982)

Annie John by Jamaica Kincaid (1985)

Breath, Eyes, Memory by Edwidge Danticat (1994)

Bone Black: Memories of Girlhood by bell hooks (1996)

Caucasia by Danzy Senna (1998)

Sugar by Bernice L. McFadden (2000)

Drinking Coffee Elsewhere by ZZ Packer (2003)

Purple Hibiscus by Chimamanda Ngozi Adichie (2003)

The Darkest Child by Delores Phillips (2004)

Daughter by Asha Bandele (2004)

Copper Sun by Sharon Draper (2006)

The Other Side of Paradise by Staceyann Chin (2009)

Before You Suffocate Your Own Fool Self by Danielle Evans
    (2010)

Akata Witch by Nnedi Okorafor (2011)

Silver Sparrow by Tayari Jones (2011)

We Need New Names by NoViolet Bulawayo (2013)

Brown Girl Dreaming by Jacqueline Woodson (2014)

Jam on the Vine by LaShonda Katrice Barnett (2015)

Ordinary Light by Tracy K. Smith (2015)

This Side of Home by Renée Watson (2015)

Under the Udala Trees by Chinelo Okparanta (2015)

The Mothers by Brit Bennett (2016)

The Sun Is Also a Star by Nicola Yoon (2016)

American Street by Ibi Zoboi (2017)

Halsey Street by Naima Coster (2017)

Here Comes the Sun by Nicole Dennis-Benn (2017)

Sing, Unburied, Sing by Jesmyn Ward (2017)

The Hate U Give by Angie Thomas (2018)

The Poet X by Elizabeth Acevedo (2018)

Genesis Begins Again by Alicia D. Williams (2019)

Girl, Woman, Other by Bernardine Evaristo (2019)

Slay by Brittney Morris (2019)

The Stars and the Blackness Between Them by Junauda Petrus
    (2019)

Such a Fun Age by Kiley Reid (2019)

Who Put This Song On? by Morgan Parker (2019)

All the Things We Never Knew by Liara Tamani (2020)

The Girl with the Louding Voice by Abi Daré (2020)

Parable of the Brown Girl: The Sacred Lives of Girls of Color by
 Khristi Lauren Adams (2020)

You Should See Me in a Crown by Leah Johnson (2020)

Black Girl, Call Home by Jasmine Mans (2021)

Chlorine Sky by Mahogany L. Browne (2021)

About the Authors

Jamaica Kincaid was born Elaine Potter Richardson in St. John's, Antigua, in May 1949. At sixteen years old, she left Antigua for New York, where she worked as an au pair and attended the New York School for Social Research. A staff writer for *The New Yorker* from 1974 to 1996, Kincaid published her first collection of short stories, titled *At the Bottom of the River*, in 1983. The debut opens with "Girl," a monologue of a mother speaking to her daughter; though it is just three pages long, this story is an unforgettable landmark of her literary career. Kincaid quickly became one of African-American literature's most influential and studied authors. Other novels include *Annie John* (1985), *Lucy* (1990), *The Autobiography of My Mother* (1996), and *Mr. Potter* (2002). Kincaid's acclaimed body of work is highly autobiographical, and often explores a variety of themes, including colonialism, motherhood, and self-discovery. Her writing earned her numerous awards, including the Anisfield-Wolf Book Award and the Lanaan Literary Award for Fiction.

Toni Morrison was born on February 18, 1931, in Lorain, Ohio. She was one of the world's most prolific and cherished authors, known for her exquisite prose, powerful use of language, and compelling depictions of Black life. Among her best-known novels are *The Bluest Eye* (1970), *Sula* (1973), *Song of Solomon* (1997), *Beloved* (1987), and *Jazz* (1992). "Recitatif" (1983) is Morrison's only published short story. It follows the lives of two young girls—one is Black and the other is white—after their mothers abruptly place them in an orphanage. Morrison never clearly identifies the race of the characters, who eventually grow up and apart.

Morrison earned her bachelor's degree in English from Howard University in Washington, D.C., in 1953 and her master's in English from Cornell University in 1955. In 1968 she moved to New York City, where she became a senior editor at Random House. While there she helped to publish books by Black writers, including Toni Cade Bambara, Gayl Jones, and June Jordan. She received a plethora of book-world accolades and honorary degrees, including the Nobel Prize in Literature in 1993 and the Presidential Medal of Freedom in 2012 from President Barack Obama.

Dorothy West was born on June 2, 1907, in Boston, Massachusetts, and discovered her writing talents early; she was just fourteen years old when her short story "Promise and Fulfillment" won a contest held by the *Boston Post*. In 1926, her story "The Typewriter" won a contest in *Opportunity* magazine, published by the National Urban League. West went to New York City to claim the award, and while there famously befriended several established writers of the Harlem Renaissance, including Zora Neale Hurston, Richard Wright, and Langston Hughes. Her signature narratives explored the realities and nuances of middle-class Black life, including *The Living Is Easy* (1948), *The Wedding* (1995), and *The Richer, the Poorer* (1995). When she died in 1998, she was the last surviving member of the Harlem Renaissance.

Rita Dove was born in Akron, Ohio, on August 28, 1952. She was the child of one of the first Black chemists to work for the US tire industry, and her parents pushed her to read widely and to study with great tenacity. Dove is best known for her complex poetry and skillful fluidity within her prose. After receiving a BA from Miami University in 1973, Dove studied German poetry at Universität Tübingen as a Fulbright Scholar, then moved on to complete her MFA at the Iowa Writers' Workshop in 1977. She published her first poetry collection, *The Yellow House on the Corner*, with Carnegie-Mellon University Press in 1980; the same press published *Thomas and Beulah* (1986), which is a loose representation of her grandparents' lives and earned her the Pulitzer Prize for Poetry. Dove had the distinction of being named poet laureate of the United States from 1993 through 1995. Famously, she was the first Black woman and the youngest at the time to hold this title.

Camille Acker is the author of the short story collection *Training School for Negro Girls*, published in 2018 with the Feminist Press. She holds a BA in English from Howard University and an MFA in creative writing from New Mexico State University. Her work has received support from the Djerassi Resident Artists Program, the Millay Colony for the Arts, Voices of Our Nations Arts Foundation, the Norman Mailer Writers Colony, and the Callaloo Creative Writing Workshop.

Toni Cade Bambara was born Miltona Mirkin Cade on March 25, 1939, and changed her name to "Toni" at six years old. Bambara was an activist, editor, writer, teacher, and documentary filmmaker. Her literary career and style were unparalleled, paying close attention to Black culture and the rhythmic vernacular of Black people, which stood out in all of her writing. Her best-known short story collection, *Gorilla, My Love* (1972), edited by Toni Morrison, unpacks themes of identity, class, and gender, while her novel *The Salt Eaters* (1980) contemplates the healing of the Black community, centering on a Black woman's recovery from a traumatizing event. In 1970, Bambara edited *The Black Woman*, an anthology of writing by emerging Black female writers, including Audre Lorde, Nikki Giovanni, Alice Walker, and more. Bambara was a friend to all Black women writers; in her poem for Toni Cade, entitled "The Making of Paper," Nikky Finney writes, "I would hunt a tree down for you."

Amina Gautier is the author of three award-winning short story collections: *The Loss of All Lost Things* (2016), whose accolades include the Chicago Public Library Foundation's 21st Century Award; *Now We Will Be Happy* (2014), winner of the Prairie Schooner Book Prize and the International Latino Book Award, among others; and *At-Risk* (2012), which won the Flannery O'Connor Award for Short Fiction. A prolific writer of short fiction, she has published over one hundred stories and won various awards for them, including the PEN/Malamud Award for Excellence in the Short Story.

Alexia Arthurs was born in Jamaica and moved with her family to Brooklyn when she was twelve. A graduate of Hunter College and the Iowa Writers' Workshop, she has published fiction in *Granta*, *The Sewanee Review*, *Small Axe*, the *Virginia Quarterly Review*, *Vice*, *Shondaland*, *Buzzfeed*, and *The Paris Review*, which awarded her the Plimpton Prize in 2017. She is the recipient of an O. Henry Prize for the story "Mermaid River." *How to Love a Jamaican* is her first book. She is a visiting assistant professor at Colby College.

Dana Johnson is the author of the short story collection *In the Not Quite Dark*. She is also the author of *Break Any Woman Down*, which won the Flannery O'Connor Award for Short Fiction, and the novel *Elsewhere, California*. Both books were nominees for the Hurston/Wright Legacy Award. Her work has been anthologized in *Watchlist: 32 Stories by Persons of Interest*, *Shaking the Tree: A Collection of New Fiction and Memoir by Black Women*, and *California Uncovered: Stories for the 21st Century*. Born and raised in and around Los Angeles, she is a professor of English at the University of Southern California.

Alice Walker was born on February 9, 1944, in Eatonton, Georgia, the youngest of eight children and the daughter of share-croppers. Walker began writing poems to soothe her childhood loneliness, favoring peaceful solitude over the business inside her home. After graduating from Sarah Lawrence College in 1965, Walker moved to Mississippi and became involved in the civil rights movement. Between 1966 and 1982, Walker wrote the essays that appear in *In Search of Our Mothers' Gardens: Womanist Prose*. The book expands on the personal and political idea of "womanism," a term coined by Walker herself. She is known for her groundbreaking novels, poems, and short stories, which offer significant insight into Black culture and intimately deal with Black womanhood. Her most famous work of fiction, *The Color Purple* (1982), won the National Book Award and made Walker the first African-American woman to win the Pulitzer Prize for Fiction.

Gwendolyn Brooks was born in Topeka, Kansas, on June 7, 1917, and raised in Chicago. She is one of the most celebrated and influential Black poets of the twentieth century. Among her many accolades, Brooks was the poet laureate for the state of Illinois for over thirty years, the first African-American Pulitzer Prize–winning author for her collection of poems entitled *Annie Allen*, and a teacher of literature across the country. She was the first Black woman to serve as consultant in poetry to the Library of Congress in 1985 and the recipient of a lifetime achievement award from the National Endowment for the Arts. Brooks took joy in learning from literature, activists, and her own and her peers' work in the community; her work reflects her deep love for Chicago, Black life, Black youth. In her poem for Paul Robeson, a Black political activist and artist, she writes, "We are each other's / magnitude and bond."

Edwidge Danticat was born on January 19, 1969, in Port-au-Prince, Haiti. Danticat took an interest in writing at the early age of nine, and later, after immigrating to the United States, turned to literature for relief from her new surroundings. In 1993, she earned her MFA from Brown University, where her thesis laid the groundwork for her first novel, *Breath, Eyes, Memory*, published by Soho Press in 1994, which later became an Oprah's Book Club selection. Danticat is a renowned author of several works of fiction, including *Claire and the Sea of Light* and *Krik? Krak!* (1995), which was awarded the Pushcart Short Story Prize, and was a finalist for the National Book Award. Danticat's work often focuses on the lives of Haitian women and addresses power dynamics, mother-daughter relationships, and the hardships of poverty. She is the recipient of the MacArthur Foundation's "Genius Award," and her work has been translated into several languages.

Shay Youngblood is a poet, fiction author, playwright, and teacher. Youngblood became an orphan early in life and was raised by a close community of family, whose likenesses show up throughout her work. Her deep understanding of injustice, which she thoroughly engages within her storytelling, began developing during her undergraduate studies at Clark Atlanta University, and later as a part of the Peace Corps. In 1993, she received an MFA in creative writing from Brown University, and soon after began teaching in programs at NYU, the University of Mississippi, and, presently, Texas A&M University. She is the author of *Shakin' the Mess Outta Misery* (1994) and *Soul Kiss* (1997), as well as a collection of short fiction titled *The Big Mama Stories* (1989), and more. Among her many honors, Youngblood has been awarded a Pushcart Prize for fiction and the Lorraine Hansberry Playwriting Award. Her plays have been widely produced and offer expansive and hopeful worlds for Black women and girls to blossom in.

Paule Marshall was born as Valenza Pauline Burke in Brooklyn on April 9, 1929, to Barbadian immigrants. At the age of twelve, she shortened her name to Paule, as a tribute to the poet

Paul Laurence Dunbar. Marshall credited her love of language to growing up and witnessing the self-affirming conversations between her mother and the many West Indian women in her life. She authored five novels, including *Praisesong for the Widow* (1983) and *The Chosen Place, the Timeless People* (1969), but is perhaps best known for her 1959 debut, *Brown Girl, Brownstones* (1959). Marshall wrote of the story "Reena": "Women of different backgrounds and of all ages and colors find that it has something to say to them about their lives. They identify with Reena . . . They love her spirit."

Zora Neale Hurston was born fifth out of eight children on January 7, 1891, in Notasulga, Alabama, to two formerly enslaved parents. Hurston grew up in Eatonville, Florida, which later would show up as the setting for several of her stories. While studying at Barnard College, she developed a great interest in ethnographic and anthropological studies. Her curiosity sent her to different countries to explore the similarities between Black life, rituals, and history. A highly honored author and Guggenheim Fellow, Hurston published numerous essays, short stories, and plays, including *Their Eyes Were Watching God* (1937), *Tell My Horse: Voodoo and Life in Haiti and Jamaica* (1983), and *Barracoon: The Story of the Last "Black Cargo"* (2018). Much of Zora Neale Hurston's recognition has been posthumous, and in 1973 Alice Walker visited Eatonville, Florida, in search of Hurston's grave site. Once found, she marked the official resting place with a headstone that affectionately reads "Genius of the South."

Credits